JE T'AIME COWBOY

Also by T.F. Rigelhof:
   A Beast With Two Backs, with Mike Mason
   The Education of J.J. Pass

Je t'aime COW BOY

T.F. RIGELHOF

GOOSE LANE

© T.F. Rigelhof, 1993.

All rights reserved. No part of this work may be reproduced or used in any form or by any means, electronic or mechanical, including photocopying, recording, or any information storage and retrieval system, without the prior written permission of the publisher.

The author's royalties will be donated, in part, to those who provide care and comfort to the juvenile victims of adult sexual delinquency.

Earlier versions of some of these stories appeared in *Canadian Fiction Magazine*, *The Journal of Canadian Fiction*, *Matrix* and *The Compass*. The story "Je t'aime, Cowboy" was adapted for television by Jerry Wexler and broadcast by CBC on the series *The Way We Are* under the title "I Love You, Cowboy."

Published with the assistance of the Canada Council, 1993.

Cover photograph by Dale McBride, 1992.
Back cover photograph by Olive Palmer, 1993.
Book design by Brenda Steeves.
Printed in Canada by The Tribune Press Ltd., Sackville, N.B.
10 9 8 7 6 5 4 3 2

Canadian Cataloguing in Publication Data

Rigelhof, T.F.
    Je t'aime cowboy
    ISBN 0-86492-144-6

I. Title.

PS8585.I419J4 1993   C813'.54   C93-098515-X
PR9199.3.R54J4 1993

Goose Lane Editions
469 King Street
Fredericton, New Brunswick
Canada E3B 1E5

For Ann, as always, and
for some of my students
and most of my friends
and all of my pals

CONTENTS

9   Hard Country Rock

23 Master Bo-Lu At Rest

49 Je t'aime, Cowboy

57 Better Days

69 A Hole With A Head In It

113 William Burroughs In Westmount

135 A Little Conversation, A Little Red Wine

151 Horses

183 Manon, Muskox, Narwhal, Owl, Polar Bear & Dylan

199 Acknowledgements

HARD COUNTRY ROCK

What would you think was about to happen if you saw a young man dressed in jeans, T-shirt, jean jacket, cowboy boots leaning up against a really great Keep-On-Trucking-type van that's black and dangerous-looking with smoked windows, oversize tires and kilos of custom chrome parked outside the service door of a restaurant at the back of a shopping plaza on a Tuesday afternoon in late September? If he's just leaning there looking casual and cool behind drop-dead sunglasses, smoking a cigarillo, would you think he's just waiting for one of the waitresses to come off the lunch shift? Would you think *So what?* and just drive on by? What would I have to tell you to get you to stop your car and park a couple of hundred feet over from him and pretend to study a road map but really watch him as he waits for the girl to appear? Would it be enough to tell you that this shopping mall is in Edmundston, New Brunswick? You do know, don't you, that east from Montreal or west from Halifax, Edmundston is always on the wrong side of the tracks? This is a town full up past overflow with the kind of guys and girls your parents and teachers said you'd become if you listened to dirty old rock'n'roll from the back seats of souped-up cars when good kids were at home doing homework, getting an education. We got educated, didn't we, and those good ol' boys with car grease under their broken fingernails and their girlfriends in the go-to-hell-in-a-hurry jeans are sort of exotic animals to us now, aren't they? And Edmundston, being home territory to them and foreign to us, is sort of a zoo where the only bars they have for the inmates are ones you get falling-down drunk in, right? So, you'll stop and watch them like the zoo-goer we've both become, won't you? What? I must have fists for brains? Let me tell you something about that young man leaning up against the van: those are his words. At this moment he is saying to himself *I must have fists for brains. This girl is going to be the kind of trouble I do not need.* The fact that he can say this to himself and still look stone dead cool is a testament to his big-city education. He is not Edmundston-born nor Edmundston-bred. He is just a stranger passing through town. Up until an hour ago, he was planning to pass straight through town without stopping even for a cup of coffee, but a pothole on the main street separated the van's muffler from the exhaust pipe. He had to get it fixed at Canadian Tire. He'd had to wait. He'd gotten a cup of coffee. What else had he gotten? He'd gotten involved with a girl, the waitress who'd served him, so what we are going to observe isn't exactly what we might have expected, that is, the undramatic ending of another workday in the lives of two young people. The young woman who is coming out through the service door right this instant is going to get something more out of what is left of this day than the hot bath and the decent dinner and couple of hours in front of the TV with her Mom that is her usual lot. She is going to get some loving!

Yes, she is! She has a glint in her eye and an anticipatory smile on her face. What else has she got? She has more style than the man with the van imagined. More style, better style. Look at her, will you? She's not at all as crude as we thought she'd be. She isn't wearing a black T-shirt with Harley-Davidson insignia or Day-Glo dirty words such as Sex Is A Lot Like Snow, You Never Know How Much You're Going To Get Or How Long It's Going To Last. She isn't wearing those go-to-hell-in-a-hurry jeans that a girl can get into only with the help of a lot of Johnson's Baby Powder, jeans that show the whole world more about the anatomy of a crotch than most of the world wants to see pressed tight against denim. She hasn't teased her hair into a Rod

Hard Country Rock

Stewart fright wig. No, she is dressed with the degree of dilapidation favoured by big-city college girls who play an insouciant kind of hide and peek with oversize plaid shirts and Levi Red Tabs and workboots and hair held in place with an elastic. The young man is so stunned that he forgets to breathe and Old Port cigarillo smoke catches in his throat and he has to clear it with a cough that is just this side of a choke.

We can sympathize. This is his first view of her as she is when she is outside the restaurant. Inside Grandma Lee's Country Kitchen, when the young man saw her for the first time in his life, she was wearing a brown gingham dress that matched the curtains and table napkins. She was also wearing a little white apron with too many frills and her hair had fallen to her shoulders in sweeping curls beneath the sort of starched cap that nurses used to wear. The young man hadn't seen her as a person at all, not even when she had looked straight at him while he ordered coffee and raisin pie. She had caught his attention by saying to him — and these are her exact words — *Hey, man, I really dig the sound of your voice. Either you're from San Antonio or you must listen to a lot of Steve Earle. I'm betting that you listen to a lot of Steve Earle.* After this, he could not take his eyes off her nor cease trying to imagine her outside the restaurant and inside his van with his cock thrusting deep inside her. In all of his twenty-some years, this young man could remember meeting only one other person outside himself on the entire planet called Earth who was actually spaced-out enough to actually say *dig* outside the contexts of gardening or coal mining. Despite his drop stone dead coolness and his van, the young man is very attentive to what gets said and how. She grabbed him with *dig* and held him with *Steve Earle*. In the past two years, he has scarcely met two dozen fans of Steve Earle. Furthermore, over the past six months, the young man has been working very hard on getting elements of Steve Earle's authentic Texas twang into his own everyday Upper Canadian voice, and not even Cindy, the girl with whom he'd been sharing an apartment in Montreal until recently and who had consequently heard a great deal of Steve Earle's authentic Texas twangy music, could hear what he desperately wanted people to hear when they heard him speak. But this waitress — she'd heard! So she'd drawn his full and total consciousness as she'd divided her attention between him and too many other customers. And when he hadn't been burning with lust for her, he'd tried to imagine who she was under the waitressing outfit and manners and what Steve Earle's music really meant to her and what might happen between them if they were to see one another somewhere else. He had thought about these things but he had not thought about rearranging things in his life so that he would actually be meeting her outside the back door of the restaurant when her workday was done. And because he had not done this and had not intended to do this, he had lusted after her in the manner of young men when they do not expect their lust to be gratified. He had lusted after her as an unconscious, insensate object. He had not meant to demean her but he had demeaned her. Repenting of this a little, he tried to find a place for her in the story he was writing — a story that was consuming him. The story thus far had taken this shape under the influence of her waitressing:

> What would you say, Bubba, if some lady sometime was to say to you that she *digs* the sound of your voice?
>
> What would you have done, Bubba?
>
> Would you have opened up a tunnel into the darker parts of your soul for her by flicking your thumb against the topmost button of your Levis and chanced a week or two of living dangerously by smiling real nice and killer-like and saying, "Do you really think so?"
>
> This was the opening I made for her. I should have blasted out the nearest exit. But I opened that tunnel, Bubba. I flicked my thumb. I smiled my killer-like smile. I said those words and that is why I'm wearing these twenty-three stitches over

my right eye and favouring my left leg. Bubba, I got to tell you, I got me a bad case of "On The Limp From Halifax Gimpy-Kneed Scars Over My Eyes Edmundston Mug Alley Blues."

The young man is not exactly a writer. He is a graduate student in a Creative Writing Programme at a Montreal university. He carries a small black notebook with him wherever he goes and fingers it frequently. This notebook contains the pet sayings of the female professor who is supervising the set of stories he is writing to fulfil the thesis part of his degree requirements. There are several pages of sentences such as *watch workers work, watch workers work until you know how to do their jobs* and *jot down what you see, not what you know.* These sentences are grouped together at the front of the notebook. He writes the various versions of his story, a story he calls "Stone Age Music," a story he intends to serve as the title piece of the collection, a story that keeps getting stalled at the first paragraph, at the end of his notebook. It took him thirty minutes and two cups of coffee after eating the raisin pie to get the current version thus far. He had been distracted by the movements of the waitress. He had tried to study the way she did her job but his cock had throbbed like Reno Kling's bass behind Steve Earle's voice and what he'd actually seen was her sort of dancing between tables, and the voice inside his head, the inner voice that was supposed to tell him what to write, had kept on reciting Steve Earle's hymn to San Antonio girls who dance by themselves beneath star-filled Texas skies.

It was then, at the precise moment that his lead paragraph had curled up and died, that the waitress had moved out of his small story and larger sexual fantasies and into his life. She'd stopped at his table with a third cup of coffee and she'd said, *Hey, man, I hope you didn't take it the wrong way, I mean like it's not that I think you're a country boy. It's like I'm really into Steve Earle, you know, and I should know better than say so because not many people are yet, you know. You probably don't even know who the hell I'm talking about, do you? You probably think he's some guy I used to date! How do you like the coffee?* And his cock had softened at the sad sigh that escaped between her words and he'd told her that he hadn't taken any offence, that, in fact, he'd been flattered since he knew exactly who Steve Earle was and was a fan of the man himself and had, in fact, been listening to *Exit O* on his way through town, which was why he hadn't noticed the biggest granddaddy of all potholes in the province and had consequently blown the muffler, which was supposed to be fixed by four o'clock. And then he had told her that he couldn't imagine finding better coffee or raisin pie elsewhere.

She'd smiled a smile that socked him in the scrotum. She'd asked, *Do you have a name I can call you?*

He'd said, *They call me Teo. T-E-O. They used to call me Theo but I got the H out of it. It's short for Theodore.* He'd said these things with a straight face even though they were lies.

She'd said, *I'm surprised they don't call you Teddy, man. You look sweet enough to be one! You don't mind my saying that, do you, Teo? You've seen pictures of Steve Earle. He's a sweet bear too. They call me Steph, short for Stephanie. I get off work at four. Will you give me a lift home? I live way out west of town and my usual ride just phoned to say she wasn't going to show up. You'd do me a favour.*

He'd done her the favour. He'd waited. We watched him wait. We saw her emerge. We gave him our sympathy as he nearly choked. We are still sympathetic, maybe even more so, because now it looks to us that she looks to him like the kind of girl with whom he could fall in love quite easily and we know from the look of her that what she wants from him is a simple good time. But we aren't altogether sympathetic: we know that he has lied to her about his name. We wonder what his next lie is going to be.

Steph takes a quick look at the van, looks him straight in the eye and says accusingly, "I thought you said you're from Texas."

Hard Country Rock

"I didn't say where I was from," Teo says.

"That's right, Teo, sorry! I guess I just think you sound so much like Steve Earle that I thought you'd said you came from Texas."

"No," he says, "I'm from southern Ontario. Originally. I live in Toronto now. I'm Teo from the big T-O. Reason I sound like a Texan, I guess, is that I used to play guitar with one of Ronnie Hawkins's bands and he wanted us to sound like a bunch of white Texas bluesmen that year, and it worked for the band and it just sort of stuck with me ever since."

She smiles as if she believes him. She is good at smiling. She half believes him. She believes the part about him coming from Ontario because his van has Ontario plates. A half-truth is fifty per cent more truth than she usually gets out of the men she meets and his lie isn't important. He probably dreamed once about playing guitar in one of Ronnie Hawkins's bands. Dreams aren't lies, not really, she thinks. She smiles because dreamers are sometimes very dreamy lovers.

And he smiles at the sight of her smile.

And she asks, "What is it?"

"An Econoline 150," he says.

"Not the van. Me! You're grinning at something about me. What?" she asks.

"Your boots," he says. "I really like your boots."

She knows that this too is a lie. He is looking at her breasts. She doesn't mind. She has lovely breasts and she knows it. Boobs. Boots. Did his tongue really slip? She bends over and straightens her laces. As she does so, she lets her shirt fall open in a way that'll let him see maximum mammary tissue. She says, "They're great, huh. They're Timberlands."

"They're what?" he asks. He is not thinking about boots. He is thinking numbers. He is thinking numbers in the high thirties.

"Timberlands," she repeats. She is not stupid. She knows where his eyes are resting. She is proud of the exercises that keep her firm, the long walks she takes in the woods in back of her mother's house. She is proud of the things she knows and the things she knows how to do. "Timberlands are the best boots you can buy and I got these across the bridge for about half of what you'd have to pay in Toronto!" she exclaims. She wishes she could stop exclaiming things to this young man but he has put an edginess on her nerves that will do her good once she is lying beside, beneath, on top of him, right side up and upside down.

"Across what bridge?" he asks. He too is nervous but his nerves are in a state that does no good for nobody nohow.

"I forgot, you're not from around here, are you, Teo? When people around here talk about crossing the bridge, they mean going to the States. Maine is just the far side of the river. Everybody from here does their serious shopping over there 'cause there is more than one way across the river and back again. But you must have heard of Timberlands, I mean, they have these really great commercials," she says as she walks around the van to the passenger side and opens the door and climbs inside.

As Teo enters from the other side and sits behind the wheel, he thinks of another Steve Earle song, one about the price a man can pay for crossing strange bridges, falling into wild rivers, living dangerously. He is afraid to sing it for her. He is growing afraid of her. He wishes he had simply kept her in the story and out of his life.

Perhaps she senses this. "Is this really your truck?" she asks.

"Here's the key," he says and holds it high.

"That's not what I mean! What I mean is, is it really yours or does it belong to someone else?"

"Why do you ask?" he asks.

"It isn't quite your style," she says.

And he resolves instantly to prove otherwise and he one-hands *Exit O* into the tape deck and fastforwards past "Nowhere Road" into the second track, and the Dukes do the intro and Reno Kling's bass guitar throbs and Teo's

Hard Country Rock

cock with it. Teo hits the accelerator and Steve Earle's surly voice sings about the hottest old Chevy in his home town and Teo overlays his own "Ford" on top of Texas Steve's "Chevy" as he reverses the van and comes very close to popping our eyes and mashing our fenders. He hangs a sharp right and we are left alone on the parking lot, listening to Steve Earle on our own playdeck singing the final verse of "Sweet Little '66."

And what, we wonder, will ever become of Teo and Steph? And this is my scenario, this is what I think will happen to them:

Behind the wheel of the Econoline 150, Teo really comes to life. He roars and pulses with life and starts putting monster moves on Edmundston's other drivers. Teo hangs an Ontario driver's red light left turn but from a middle lane and cuts off a local badass in a pride-of-the-whole-fuckin'-block Camaro. I'll give Teo great reflexes and the Econoline a great engine so that nothing gets bent except Steph's ear as Badass Camaro pulls alongside her at the next set of lights and tells her to tell her boyfriend a whole lot of things that not even a girl in go-to-hell-in-a-hurry jeans and a Harley-Davidson T-shirt deserves to hear.

Ever the graduate student, Teo records seventeen distinct uses of *fuck* in a variety of forms in Badass's forty-five-second monologue. And what is his answer? His answer is to give Badass the big finger and then swing in behind the Camaro after the light change and ride it the length of the block, tailgating, tailgating, tailgating the whole block. And then Teo pulls out and passes Badass on the right and gives him the big finger again as he swings back in front and leaves the man jammed up against his brake pedal sucking in exhaust fumes and burned rubber.

Steph is very quiet through all of this. Finally she says, "You really shouldn't do things like that around here. These guys in their Camaros take themselves very seriously. We'd better get out of here fast before he gets back with a whole lot of his friends." And then she tells Teo where to turn and they are off the main highway and onto a secondary road that follows the contours of the land in a narrow ribbon of badly cracked and poorly patched asphalt and meanders through countryside that's almost postcard scenic and then the hedgerow disappears on the left and the road on which they are travelling runs parallel to the new highway and the new highway is packed with six or seven Camaros and Teo loses his nerve and Steph loses her way and tells him to take a turn and they are on a logging trail and — scrunch — the new muffler is flattened by a rock in the roadbed and the van is making noises that are dead giveaways. Teo backs up into a stand of trees and kills the engine.

They sit and listen. They hear cars roar past the entrance to the logging road and ten minutes later they hear the same cars roar past in the opposite direction. And then it is very quiet and Teo can feel the throb of exhilaration in his cock that comes with safety at the end of an adventure, and he clambers into the back of the van and invites Steph to join him in sharing a bottle of Southern Comfort and Steph takes a small toke of stone good hash from the inside of her workboot, and they drink and they smoke and I think I'll let her get the things she took the ride in the hope of getting. I'll let her have her loving. I'll let her rock and roll his body and hers with nice soft meaningless sex, mindless, carefree sex. I don't mind. I really don't mind. I can let go of them right here and now. I can let them discover for themselves if there is some mystery in the fusion of their bodies that is going to surface and erupt between them and lead them to love. I can do it without suffering the pangs of jealousy. How about you? You say that people like this are born for big trouble? What kind of trouble do you want to give them? You want me to imagine it for you, do you? You think that because I asked you to stop and observe what was happening I have a duty to take you to the end of the story? Okay, but remember, this is your idea and not mine, your scena-

Hard Country Rock

rio not mine: as the earth begins to move for the lovers, the van begins to shake. It's not the vibrations of love. It's not a broken shock absorber. It's Badass and the Camaro gang and they are doing their very best to overturn the van with the lovers inside it. Teo is angry, hell-bent-for-self-destruction angry. He picks up a tire iron.

Steph says, "Put it away. We'll have to outwit them. They've got the muscles. We've got the brains." And then she wiggles her bare bottom back into her jeans and we are glad that she wears her jeans loose enough to do it in a hurry, aren't we? She slides her shirt back over her head onto outstretched arms. She undoes a couple more buttons. She whispers her game plan in Teo's ear.

Steph positions herself at the side door like a lineman in a game of touch football. At her signal, Teo pulls back the door. Steph's shirt is open wide enough and her breasts large and white and firm enough to hold and pop the eyeballs of the nearest two Camaro Badasses. Steph kicks high and hard and connects with the lower balls of the one nearest the door. There is screaming, writhing and swearing and Steph is above it all, leaping high in the air like a dancer and landing with a ten-foot jump start to the edge of the woods. Teo is behind her running close to the ground and swinging the tire iron and connecting with a knee, and there is louder screaming and more writhing and the kind of cursing that takes a lot of practice to get just so right. And they flee to the woods and they make love in a haystack until morning comes. No? You think they have more trouble coming to them than this, do you? You're probably right. Guys like Teo can never run as fast as the women they chase, can they. Teo gets caught and a couple of hours pass and we'll pass over them in silence and pick up the tale with Steph finding her way back to the place where the van had been parked.

As she steps out of the woods, she sees Teo in the clearing she bounded with one leap. He is illuminated by a blood-red moon as fat as a balloon. He is stretched out on a shingle of rock, resting his head on his left elbow. He is naked and white in the moonlight and looks very much like a piece of classical statuary except that his posture is not entirely passive and he does have a penlight between his teeth and a ballpoint pen in his hand and he is writing in his notebook.

"They've gone?" Steph asks.

Teo nods his head and the little beam of his electric light moves through a small arc.

"Where's the van?" she asks

Teo points his pencil of light towards the far edge of the clearing. It does not penetrate the darkness but Steph sees the glint of moonlight on chrome. She goes over to investigate. Teo continues writing.

"Boy, they really trashed it, didn't they!" she exclaims. "How are we ever going to get it out of there?"

Teo doesn't bother to answer. The fate of the van no longer interests him. He is consumed by the story he is writing.

"Are you okay?" she asks. "What did they do to you? I figured they might hurt you less if I wasn't around to watch it, you know. Guys like that are crueller when they're trying to impress women. I hope they didn't hurt you too much. But I did stay long enough to see them take your clothes. That's when I headed back home and got these for you. I figured we'd be all night looking for yours." And she walks to him and hands him clothes in a bundle.

He ignores them. He keeps writing.

Steph touches his flesh. It is very cold. "You should have crawled back into the bushes. It's warmer next to the earth," she says as she removes her hand from his leg. "You'd better get into these as quickly as you can. They should just about fit you. The guy I was living with until a couple of months ago was about your size."

Teo has finished his final paragraph. He puts down his pen. He tries to put on the socks she has brought. His fingers are so stiff that Steph has to pull the socks over his feet. And then she has to help him into green cotton

Hard Country Rock

workpants and shirt, a sleeveless thermal vest and a pair of running shoes. As she dresses him, Steph says, "I'll build a campfire and you can get warmed up a bit before we walk back to my place. It's only a couple of miles. My Mom is making us something hot to eat for when we get back. She's really a good cook too. She's the one who bakes the raisin pies we serve at that place where I work."

Her words do not rouse him. He is still in the grip of his story. He is still sifting through the various strands of it, checking for loose ends. The van poses a problem that he isn't certain he has successfully resolved. Should he leave it where it lies or should he hold out the promise of a tow truck coming in the morning to retrieve it? A tow truck could do the job in his story. Literature is not the same as life. The van in his life has been gutted by fire and lies at the bottom of a ten-foot ravine. It would require some kind of crane to remove it, so it will probably just stay where it is until parts of it are looted and others just rust away. That is the wrong image for what he wants to say. He decides to insert a tow truck at the appropriate place. He turns his story over once more.

Steph has gathered some fallen branches and broken them and piled them on the rock upon which he sits. She has gathered some pine cones and twigs and made a mound out of them beneath the branches. Satisfied with her woodsmanship, she takes out her matches. She sees that she only has a couple. She'll need to make some tinder to get the fire started with a single match. What she needs is some paper. She spies his notebook. She asks him, "Can I take a couple of pages out of this?"

Teo doesn't answer. He is still lost in his story. She picks up the notebook and grasps it firmly and does what? Do you want her to tear out blank pages? It would only take her an extra moment. Or do you want me to have her tear out the last two pages from his story? Do you remember how much trouble he had starting it? Does he deserve to be robbed of its ending now? You think he does? Is it that you hate guys who write stories that have guys called

Bubba in them? Or is it that you hate him? You really shouldn't hate him. You scarcely know him. You would never have met him at all if I hadn't waved you over to this parking lot and asked you to keep me company in this Maritime zoo. I know him very well and I don't hate him. I don't hate him even though I followed him all the way from Montreal to Halifax as he went chasing after Cindy, even though she has made it clear to him that she no longer wants to have anything to do with him and I have made it clear to him that I do want him to live with me, at least until his stories are written. I know I can help him write them. I know his supervisor very well. I know exactly what she wants from his stories. I know precisely what she wants from him. I know she will leave him alone when he wants to be alone. I know she will listen to Steve Earle songs with him when that is what he wants. She'll listen to them the way Cindy never listened to them. She'll listen to one right now just as soon as I hit the button and fade away and leave him singing about a road that leads nowhere but always brings you back to where you started from.

MASTER BO-LU AT REST

The big yellow taxi idled noisily at the curb outside École St. Léon de Westmount. The driver stared dumbly at the nickel and dime in the palm of his hand. "*Merci* bloody much, tightass," he mumbled as he shovelled the tip into his jeans pocket. Then he shrugged, admiring the thin ankles of the lady he had just deposited. He watched her smooth the line of her peach Courrèges sweater over her camel skirt as she regarded herself in the glass door of the school, then disappeared inside. She did not look back. He was beneath her notice. "*C'est la vie*," he sighed, "teachers aren't what they used to be."

The driver shrugged a second time. It felt good. He heaved his shoulders, relaxed his arm muscles, released the fatigue of a night's driving. As he resettled himself behind the wheel, he took a wristwatch from his shirt pocket and checked the time. The watch was a battered old Timex with a broken bracelet; the hands on the dial read eight-thirty-five. He subtracted five minutes. It was not a very accurate watch. But as he replaced it in his shirt pocket, the driver thought of the value of this timepiece and smiled. It was not yet the middle of the month and already seven customers had tipped him the price of a new bracelet. It amused him that so many of his passengers were moved to generosity by his empty wrist. It seemed to violate one of their deeper sensibilities. His smile broadened into a grin that collapsed into a yawn and with that yawn he surveyed the street looking for one last fare, someone he could drop off on his way home.

The west side of the street, as he scanned it, was full of kiddies on their way to school. A couple of people were walking dogs, letting them shit right where the little ones would be sure to tramp. He looked away in disgust. On the other side of the street, two men were standing on the sidewalk, lost in conversation. Then one looked up, saw the taxi, flagged him. The driver slipped his car into gear, drove past them fifty feet, wheeled into a driveway, backed out and pulled up alongside. They kept talking, ignored his presence. The driver turned on his meter and watched them through his wing mirror. He could see only one of their faces, the face of the one who was doing all the listening. Something stirred in his memory, made him catch his breath. He knew that he knew the man. It was a face from the distant past. He closed his eyes and waited for an image to form in the middle of his forehead. But he drew a blank.

His rear door opened, then closed. He opened his eyes. A voice said, "Montreal General, *s'il vous plaît*."

"*Urgence?*" the driver asked.

"*Non*. Outpatients," the voice replied, wavering over the Anglicism.

The driver rammed down the accelerator. As the car lept forward, the driver noticed that he had only one passenger, that the man whose face he was trying to place had not gotten into the car but was walking along the street behind them. He felt his passenger's eyes boring a hole into the back of his neck.

"Not so fast. It isn't so urgent."

The driver maintained his speed, composed his face into a yawn and looked into the rearview mirror. All he saw was a slightly soiled bandage taped diagonally across the left ear, framed by wisps of oily hair.

The passenger noticed. "*Une infection de mes oreilles. Je n'ai pas lavé mes cheveux pour deux semaines.*" The accent was tortured.

"It's okay," the driver said. "You can speak English to me, okay. Your ear still hurts? I had an earache once. It felt like all my teeth were falling out."

"Yes, I know exactly what you mean. The pain is gone now. Just an itch. But my hair! What a mess! *Mais si vous préférez, je vais parler français. Vous êtes un séparatiste?*"

The passenger poked a bony forearm across the back of the seat and pointed to the Parti Québécois decal on the dashboard. The gesture brought his face into clearer view in the mirror. It was a long thin face, rather horsey, with a prominent nose and heavy drooping eyelids. The driver had a moment's uncertainty as to whether the face belonged to a man or a woman; the bluish shadow along the cheeks tipped the balance. "Me a separatist? No, back on the fifteenth of November, I'm taking these people to the Paul Sauvé Arena to celebrate the election victory. This one guy, he slaps that sticker on the dash. It stays there. The tips are better." The driver made a practice of telling his customers what they didn't want to hear. This guy, he thought, wanted to hear the English kicked, wanted to sympathize. He wasn't going to do it, not for him, not today. "What you want to do when you wash your hair is to pack your ear with cotton wool covered with Vaseline. Keeps them really dry. The doctor should have told you that."

The driver turned his attention to the road, nosed the yellow car into Côte des Neiges, eyed the onrushing traffic, gunned the taxi across two lanes, made a violent left turn, and merged into the first of two streams ascending the mountain. He edged his car into the innermost lane and stayed put all the way up to the hospital entranceway. He wasn't in a mood to play games with other drivers. And he was preoccupied. He was still trying to remember the name to put to the face of his passenger's friend.

As he pulled up at the doors of the hospital, he said, "Remember now what I said about Vaseline and cotton wool. It works. I know."

"Thanks. I'll try it or at least ask the doctor about it. Thanks again." The passenger gathered himself up.

"Hey," the driver said, "that guy you were talking to, he looked sort of familiar. Who is he?"

"I'm quite certain you wouldn't know him," the passenger said primly and rather defensively as he flounced out of the back seat.

When he was halfway to the doors and in the middle of a throng of nurses, the driver sang out, "Remember, lots and lots of Vaseline. Makes it much easier."

The nurses tittered. "It's for his ears, you understand," the driver shot back. The nurses tittered some more. The horsey-faced man hurried through the hospital doors. The commissionaire waved for the driver to move on. He did.

It was while he was drifting back down the mountain that the driver identified the man he had not remembered. As he closed his eyes to shake off some spots that were forming from the sunlight glaring off chromed metal onto his tired retinas, the blackness behind his eyeballs broke apart like curtains in a theatre and a tableau composed itself and then dissolved. In the instant of its existence, he saw and recognized four young men seated at a heavy wooden table playing a hand of bridge. The contract was for a grand slam in spades. They were playing the tenth trick. The man he had seen in Westmount was losing an unnecessary finesse against his own jack of diamonds. A honking horn forced the driver's eyes open. The tableau vanished but somewhere in the back of his head he began to remember that it had been 1967, May, Saturday afternoon, Ottawa, Main Street, the University Seminary, the recreation room. Space and time came back in a rush. Another horn, another set of lights. His inner voice gave a name to each of the card players: the one he wanted to remember was Everett Fredericks. Everett Fredericks. How could he have forgotten! As he drove, the voice inside his head rumbled on, filling in miscellaneous details of that long ago afternoon, odd little facts about their clothes, their cigarettes, the pattern of the Aviator playing cards they had used over and over and over again, the exact shape and colour and texture of the tartan carpet slippers he had been wearing that day.

The driver did his best to ignore this flotsam of appearance and jetsam of texture that was so much a part of his ability to recall things totally, the ability that made him an actor gifted enough to pass as just another hack whenever he felt the need to escape from being himself. At the moment he did not want such details, he wanted to remember only the things that had once connected him to Everett Fredericks and Fredericks to him and both of them to the seminary in Ottawa. But the emotions of that time and place would not return to him apart from the minutiae of the lives they had led together, their card games, their cigarettes, the songs they had listened to over and over again on the portable stereo in the recreation room, out of earshot of the classical music fanatics with their heavy duty stereo and serious manner down the corridor. Those songs rushed through his head: Bob Dylan brought it back home again with "Maggie's Farm" and "Gates Of Eden" and "It's All Over Now, Baby Blue." The driver closed his eyes, shook his head, tried to break free of Dylan's rasping voice. But he could not. The black space in his head filled up with the images of that album cover: Dylan holding a small grey kitten in the foreground, a movie magazine, a woman in a red dress, a bunch of scattered record albums, a portable fallout shelter in a yellow cardboard box, a picture of Lyndon B. Johnson on the cover of *Time*, a fireplace.

The driver opened his eyes just in time to avoid a collision. Then, by concentrating on the name Everett Fredericks and repeating it over and over again, he matched the sound of that name to the rhythm of the traffic flowing around him. It made a nice little song in his head, a mantra of sorts. So he sang it all the way home, wondering all the while what Everett Fredericks would think of him now that he — Adrian (Bolo) Boileau of Regina, Saskatchewan — was the follower of a different god, was a veritable cardinal in his own right, a guru, Master Bo-Lu of The Universal Fellowship Of Maya Redeemers. He wondered if Ev Fredericks would laugh or cry or simply think he was off his head. It was a question that he could not answer. Fredericks had always had his own way of seeing things. But beyond that, he — Adrian (Bolo) Boileau — wasn't altogether certain that he could answer the question himself.

Home for Adrian (Bolo) Boileau a.k.a. Master Bo-Lu of The Universal Fellowship Of Maya Redeemers was a newly renovated building in midtown Montreal. One of a long row of nearly identical brick townhouses, its character had been much altered over the course of the twentieth century. It had declined from a spacious private home in a nice residential district into a nice rooming house in a street of rooming houses in the forties and fifties, and then it had degenerated into a squalid refuge for transients and flower children in the sixties. In the early seventies it had been sold to a land developer who failed in his bid to demolish it to erect yet another high-rise apartment building. And so it had stood — abandoned, uninhabited and unloved, subject to periodic small fires — for half a dozen years until The Universal Fellowship Of Maya Redeemers acquired it on the cheap from its mortgage holder. The UFMR, as it was familiarly known, had turned the lowest floor into a vegetarian restaurant, the second floor into a boutique packed with cheap Asian imports, the third floor into meeting rooms, library and bookstore for its own devotees. The topmost floor was made over into a small residence for those members of The Fellowship who conducted its services, gave its lectures, ran its boutique and restaurant and operated its two yellow taxicabs. As such, the building more or less fit into its neighbourhood, which had in recent years become an annex to Concordia University.

    Boileau swung the taxi into one of the parking spaces behind the building. He honked twice. Before the sound had faded, a young man with long auburn hair and a full beard of much lighter colour emerged through the back door. This young man wore a loose-fitting purple shirt and orange corduroy trousers. He held a bowl of rice and ate rapidly from it with his fingers. As the young man ate, Boileau removed his own identity card from the sun visor, toted up the mileage on the odometer and the number of fares on the meter, emptied the coin changer on the dashboard and entered several series of figures in a small black notebook. He gathered up his leather windbreaker and his mirrored sunglasses from the seat beside him and got out, digging the heels of his cowboy boots into the loose crushed stone. The young man held the door open for him. Boileau dropped a set of keys into the outstretched hand. "Wash and wax it before you take it out again. And vacuum the inside. Now. And remember to finish your breakfast inside and on time after this."

The young man bowed his head and shuffled his feet. His lips moved silently.

Boileau pushed past, bounded up the back staircase two steps at a time. At the third landing he stopped, checked his pulse, opened a door marked Private and stepped inside.

Boileau stood in a panelled dressing room. He saw his reflection in the mirror wall to his left. He looked away, pulled off his boots, his checked shirt, his jeans, his underwear. He dropped everything in a jumble. Then, stripped of the clothes that identified him as an ordinary working man, he pulled sharply with both hands at his hair. The whole mass of brown shaggy curls came away from shaved and polished skull. Boileau flung the wig on top of the clothes, stepped past it, studied his naked image in the mirror. It pleased him.

The pleasure he took in the sight of himself was merited. His was a genuine handsomeness: he was of middle height and well-proportioned, long in the limbs, slender in the waist, round-bottomed, broad-shouldered. There was not an excess ounce on him, and his skin gleamed with a uniform golden tan. His shaven head gave strength and severity to his beauty and drew attention to his face, a face which did not transmit the blankness of a fun-lover. His eyes were blue ice and deeply recessed. Against the brown of his face they radiated a powerful intensity, a seriousness that had creased the skin sharply between his eyes. His face itself was angular, dominated by sharp high cheekbones and a finely chiselled nose that gave him a vaguely oriental look. Some said that he looked like Pierre Elliott Trudeau but the resemblance was superficial. Boileau's looks were less patrician, less boyish, more cunning. Smiling broadly, he pulled open one panel of the mirror and stepped inside the bathroom beyond it.

Boileau turned on the taps and began running a bath. As he waited for the tub to fill, he plugged in an electric shaver and began stroking his face. He knew his face well and shaved it with automatic motions that slowed, then stopped altogether as he reached the area above his ears. He was still a novice in the art of shaving his own scalp and found it a ticklish business. And when he was tickled, he giggled foolishly. He had found that he could maintain his composure only by not looking in the mirror. So he bent low over the basin as if he was washing his hair rather than removing all trace of it. Bent low like this, he noticed a bit of red paper protruding from the toilet. He turned off the shaver. Then, taking a deep breath, he reached down and raised the seat. A small red envelope was affixed to the underside with a strip of cellotape. Boileau removed the tape and held the envelope in his hand for a moment before opening it and withdrawing the single sheet of paper.

The paper was the same shade of red as its envelope. It was folded in thirds and sealed with a globule of golden wax imprinted with the logogram of The Fellowship — the letters U, F, M and R emerging singly from the

mouths of a four-headed dragon. With a deep sigh, Boileau broke the seal and read what was written:
Bo-Lu
Me cuvtiv fuoe
Odzins
It fvn H
Sam-Kr.

At that moment, Boileau missed having a head of hair to scratch. He contented himself by massaging his scalp as he puzzled over the message inscribed in the altogether too familiar hand of the founder of The Universal Fellowship Of Maya Redeemers. The message made no sense. He sighed a second time but this sigh had a note of relief in it. Boileau taped the sheet to the wall just above the bathtub faucets where he could study it as he bathed.

In the hierarchy of UFMR, Bolo Boileau as Master Bo-Lu ranked second. He was Protector Of All Redeemers. According to the Civil Statutes of the Province of Québec governing the incorporation of companies and societies, he was the vice-president of The Fellowship and CEO of the various companies through which it controlled the restaurant, the boutique, the two taxis, some real estate and a printing shop. But according to his own lights, he was now the only one who stood between The Fellowship and chaos. These lights had guided him in recent weeks to take his title at face value and to wrest control bit by bit from the hands of its founder and legal president, the Venerable Swami Sam-Kr.

Swami Sam-Kr was not easily deposed. His grip upon The Fellowship had been so absolute that Boileau had to resort to a series of stratagems that would have pleased Machiavelli and sent even the rawest of police constables scurrying after dossiers on confidence men. Luckily for Boileau, no one in The Fellowship read very much or befriended policemen. Even so, it had not been clear sailing: Swami Sam-Kr was never to be completely counted out for the very good reason that he possessed a queer genius. Until Boileau's arrival, UFMR had been the total and complete creation of this one man. It was Swami Sam-Kr who had perceived in his own name — Samuel Kerr — two Sanskrit root syllables, *sam* meaning "together" and *kr* meaning "make"; this perception made him realize that he had a destiny beyond the one conferred upon him by his family, friends and the society of which they were leading commercial representatives. They had always thought of him merely as a new pillar for the business community and a potential political property to be moulded by sure hands to manifest the principles of the Progressive Conservative Party and serve its ends. He and only he had ever perceived within himself the capacity to make something entirely new of himself. And in Boileau's eyes this certified him as a genius. For Boileau, it was almost unimaginable that anyone who had been born and raised in the Upper Westmount world of Samuel Kerr could still have the capacity to see beyond its privileged borders. For Boileau, such a thing was as unlikely as Abram seeing beyond Ur of the Chaldees, Moses seeing beyond Egypt, Jesus seeing beyond Nazareth, Mahomet seeing beyond Medina. And so Boileau revered Samuel Kerr as a real Swami, as one who could see in others a capacity to be *samnyasim,* that is, ones who renounce all else in the pursuit of true destiny. Boileau regarded this as true genius because it had drawn him outside himself, something that not even the Holy Roman Catholic Church, with all of its wealth, prestige, history and sanctity, had been capable of doing. For Boileau, the only justification for deposing this great man was the belief that Swami Sam-Kr had begun to betray that genius and the followers it had drawn to itself.

Before Boileau had begun to act as Master Bo-Lu, he had asked himself over and over again how he, who did not possess a similar genius, could judge Sam-Kr's and detect its malfunctions. These scruples ended abruptly when Swami Sam-Kr suddenly demanded that he oversee the liquidation of UFMR assets. Master Bo-Lu was not convinced that it was only through throwing off the bonds of physical wealth that The Fellowship could regain its original innocence and rise to new heights. And so Master Bo-Lu had turned away from Swami Sam-Kr, something that he had thought impossible, for he could not and would not break everything apart, tear down all that had been brought together bit by bit, piece by piece, member by member, throughout the life of UFMR, and given to him to protect. Master Bo-Lu had seen immediately that the best he could do was to persuade Swami Sam-Kr to go into retreat for some months and thereby generate the appropriate spiritual climate so necessary in the circumstances. Sam-Kr's withdrawal gave Master Bo-Lu a relatively free hand. But that freedom, he realized, could not seem absolute to the others. Knowing the dangers that lie in wait for leaders of palace coups, Master Bo-Lu saw that spiritual communion had to be maintained between Swami and his disciples in some way, but in a way that he could regulate. So he had turned Swami Sam-Kr into an oracle who could be consulted by any devotee but interpreted only by himself. The results had been these bits of red paper with their odd messages.

The one he now considered was the second to last he intended to receive. After this, there would be only one more question and one final answer, an answer leading to a referendum among The Fellowship's members that would surrender everything into Master Bo-Lu's keeping. In turning Swami Sam-Kr into an oracle, Boileau planned to drive him over the edge into complete madness, the sort of madness that led to powers-of-attorney being acted upon. In the jumble of letters taped to the wall, he saw the evidence of his success. Deprived of audible contact with his disciples, Swami Sam-Kr had been forced to commune with his own spirits. To gain greater access, he had employed a Ouija board and fallen into raptures of incomprehensibility. By persuading both questioner and oracle that he understood and could interpret these utterances, Master Bo-Lu had progressively weakened Swami Sam-Kr's hold upon both his disciples and his own sanity. As Boileau stared at this message, he began to impose an interpretation on the words that would advance his goal: a referendum he could not lose. When he finally saw in them what he wanted to see, he began to sing Dylan's "Lay Lady Lay" and scrub away the night's dirt.

When Master Bo-Lu emerged from the bathroom, a white towel wrapped around his waist, his skin glowing and spicy with scent, his dressing room was again well-ordered. While he bathed, an unseen hand had sorted out his work clothes, hung them on hangers, placed his soiled underclothes in a laundry hamper and brushed his wig before mounting it on the styrofoam block in its cabinet. This hand had also laid out a pair of fresh white pyjama bottoms, a pair of black silk slippers and a Japanese kimono in black silk embossed over the heart with the logogram of the four-headed dragon. A thick black exercise mat and a sun lamp had also been set up for him in the middle of the dressing room. Master Bo-Lu removed the towel from his loins, prostrated himself upon the mat and began performing a series of gentle stretching exercises. His movements became more rapid and complex until he concluded with a series of thirty-five ordinary push-ups. Then he dried the sweat from his skin, laid himself flat out on the mat, set the timer on the sun lamp and toasted his body for five minutes on each side.

With the sun lamp switched off, he rested on his mat, observing his surroundings. The floor was carpeted with a very thick, very large, very rich Indian rug woven of silk and wool in shades of green and gold and white. The walls of the dressing room, except for the one that was of mirror, were panelled with fine old mahogany that a member of The Fellowship had salvaged from the library of a demolished Sherbrooke Street mansion. One wall was draped with a tapestry portraying the four-headed dragon that UFMR had taken as its ruling symbol. The dragon was deep red and gold against a background of bottle green. Handmade by four of The Fellowship's members, the tapestry was bold and slightly primitive in contrast to the refined workmanship in the rug. On the wall opposite the tapestry, one of the panels was ajar, revealing a walk-in closet. From where he lay, Master Bo-Lu could observe the line of clothes and the row of footwear arranged in three distinct groups: the jeans and sneakers and cowboy boots and windbreakers he wore when he drove taxi and recruited members for The Fellowship, the kimonos and pyjamas and slippers he wore when he instructed devotees, the tailored suits and shirts and handmade boots he wore when he attended to business interests. All these things gave him a strong sense of self-satisfaction. But the room held more than this; it contained many things that made him feel secure. There was a low, richly brocaded sort of settee piled high with cushions. There were two black lacquered chinoiserie chairs inlaid with mother-of-pearl and a cabinet that matched. There were lovely low tables of carved wood and engraved brass. And everywhere there were objets d'art, tall Chinese vases and copper Indian ewers and statues of bronze, wood and stone, as well as small ivories and pieces of jade and incense pots and scrolls and screens, enough to rival the collection of one of Montreal's finer galleries of Oriental art. Looking at these things, Master Bo-Lu knew The Fellowship was a success, for each and every one of them had been given by followers and friends. Happy, immersed in this sense of things, he rose from his mat, dressed and left the room to take up his duties, the duties that would make all these things his very own.

As Master Bo-Lu entered the adjoining room that served as the central office of UFMR, two young women rose to greet him. The younger of the two was the quicker to rise and to bow low before him. She was just barely a woman, little more than a girl, and she nursed a very small, very red baby at her breast in an inexperienced way. Master Bo-Lu acknowledged both mother and child with a slight bow of his own and motioned them back to their seat on a cushion on the floor. When they were again seated, he bent low over the mother and peered at the baby. Its eyes were closed and impassive as its mouth tugged furiously at its mother's breast, trying to swallow it whole. Master Bo-Lu extended his hand to the infant and stroked the back of its head. The baby, startled, squirmed beneath the pressure of his hand and lost hold of the nipple. It balled its little fingers into fists and shook them, letting loose a howl of rage. He stood his ground and stroked the baby a second time while its mother replaced her breast in its mouth. Master Bo-Lu removed his hand from the infant and placed it gently on the mother's head. He moved her head forward very gently and kissed it from above. It was a lingering kiss that allowed him to take a long look at the idle breast hanging heavily inside her loose blouse. He tried to imagine the taste of mother's milk within his own mouth and inwardly cursed Swami Sam-Kr for prohibiting sexual intercourse during times of lactation. He looked again at the infant and its enjoyment of the thing that was forbidden him. The sight repulsed him. He was glad the child was Swami Sam-Kr's and not his own. In that moment of revulsion, he decided also that he might do well to alter some of the sexual decrees of The Fellowship and depose the Swami's hold on this young mother's heart.

But that moment of inner decision was ended by a light cough from the second woman in the office. Master Bo-Lu had not yet acknowledged her bow to him. The light cough was meant to remind him of this. He turned to her and bowed carelessly. Acknowledged now by her master, she rose to her full height and said, "Thérèse, see to the Master's room."

The young mother rose from her cushion and backed out of the room, bowing low over her child.

Left now to themselves, Master Bo-Lu and the woman eyed each other warily. In the hierarchy of The Universal Fellowship Of Maya Redeemers, she ranked third, just below Master Bo-Lu. Her name was Helena and she was called Mother by the devotees and secretary-treasurer on the letterheads of UFMR businesses. Helena was a very efficient secretary-treasurer and a very modern mother. Not the least matronly, she was tall, slim, angular, full of unresolved tensions that somehow did not lessen or weaken an overpowering determination. She was grim and her grimness gave her jaw a severity that turned down the ends of an otherwise sensual mouth, robbing the lips of fullness and colour. The tension by which she was held captive, the tension that Swami Sam-Kr had increased by elevating Master Bo-Lu above her, pinched her eyes, held them close to her nose in the narrow focus, exaggerated their blackness and reduced their glow to a single harsh gleam. That gleam wilted Master Bo-Lu. He could not out-stare it. He looked away from her face and in looking away failed to meet her challenge. He knew that he would never overpower her strength. But he could undermine her weaknesses. As he backed away, he assumed a clinical interest in her hand, which was bandaged. "How's the hand today?" he asked.

"Oh, it isn't quite so stiff as it was last night. I soaked it in cold water for an hour or so and that loosened it up a bit. But it still throbs."

"Let me rebandage it." Her answer gave him the upper hand. She was obsessed with her health.

"You needn't." But she automatically opened the drawer of her desk in which she kept a small tin box with scissors and gauze and adhesive tape.

Master Bo-Lu made her sit in her office chair at her desk and extend her arm along the desk's surface. He snipped away the tape that held the dressing in place and unrolled the strip of gauze slowly and with great care. There was deftness to his touch. Competent as any doctor on television, he inspected the soft new skin that had grown over the place between her index and neighbouring finger that had been lacerated. He held her hand in his and stroked it therapeutically, massaging the flesh, working the tendons, exercising the muscles. Then he rewrapped it. When he was done, his bandaging looked professional.

There was silence between them as he worked, a silence punctuated only by the sound of her breathing, which grew soft and steady as he worked. When he had finished, she said, "You do great bandaging. Were you ever in medical school?"

"Not in this life."

"No. Of course not but, well, I sometimes think you must have been a physician in a previous incarnation."

"And you, I think you were once a dancer."

"Why do you say that? Do you know I spent my entire childhood wanting to be a ballerina! I've never mentioned this to anyone except Swami. Did he tell you this about me?"

Master Bo-Lu did not answer. He sensed from her interest that he might yet find a way to will her to submission. So he smiled his softest smile and changed the subject. "Josef was still eating breakfast when I arrived home this morning. He is to wash, wax and clean the cars daily as penance until I instruct otherwise."

"His eating. That was his rebellion against me. I chastised him last night. He was in Thérèse's room at two o'clock. I found him. He tried to tell me that he had gone to check on the baby."

"Did you speak to Thérèse about it?"

"She was sound asleep. The baby was awake but content. I don't think he touched her. You know, these things wouldn't happen if you stayed at home at night instead of chasing around in that taxi. I really don't see the point of it. It's not as if you had to drive the cab, recruit in that way. Our best members find their way to us by themselves. Your time is too valuable. What's the point of being out there when we need you here?"

At moments like this Master Bo-Lu understood why Swami Sam-Kr had given her the title of Mother. He bit the inside of his lip to keep from answering. Silence, he knew, was his most effective weapon with her. But silence was very difficult. He longed to confide in a woman, to share the burdens of his holy office, to divulge to someone just how necessary it was to his own sanity to escape from The Fellowship for at least a part of each day and to live a little as he used to in the realm of ordinary people.

"I'm sorry," Helena said with finality when it became clear that Master Bo-Lu had no intention of responding to her complaints. "I'm being a nag and I know it. You have your reasons and I've no right to challenge them. You do as you must. It's just that we all feel so vulnerable late at night now that Swami is no longer among us in his body. I know his spirit protects us but we don't always feel the strength of that presence."

Master Bo-Lu nodded sagely. "I know," he said, "it's difficult. Perhaps it will be best if Josef leaves here. He's not reliable. Send him to the farm. He can herd the goats. Now, let's see the accounts."

Helena smiled wanly as she unlocked the metal filing cabinet and brought out the ledgers of UFMR's various enterprises.

Helena was a gifted accountant. She mothered figures with absolute self-confidence. And so it was that Master Bo-Lu passed the next couple of hours very pleasantly. The room, airy and spacious, offset the claustrophobia Master Bo-Lu normally felt in the presence of mathematical calculations. His own sense of economics was instinctive, intuitive, and the rational consideration of credits and debits imposed upon him a burden that for most of his life he had found unbearable. But Helena had changed this. She held the mechanics of accountancy — the ledgers, the account books, the balance sheets — much as a musician holds her instrument, and she played fine melodies upon them until each melody merged with the others in a harmonious whole. He admired her performances and profited from them. And this day her technique was especially fine as she illustrated how each of the several business interests had increased its equity and profits over the preceding period. Swami Sam-Kr's retreat into solitude had served some good purpose beyond whatever spiritual enlightenment or madness it worked in his soul. It had allowed Master Bo-Lu to rid UFMR of losing propositions and consolidate its strengths. Master Bo-Lu felt a wonderful sense of relief and accomplishment at the absence of red ink.

As Helena tidied her desk and replaced the various files and journals and notebooks in the safe confines of steel cabinets, Master Bo-Lu kept his eyes on her. Of all the members of The Fellowship, Helena was the one he respected most. But he feared her as well. There was simply too much about her that he could not comprehend. He admired her self-sufficiency and could not reconcile her vulnerability with it. He knew how to manipulate her responses to him but could not be certain what sort of emotions his manipulations stirred inside her. Whatever she felt towards him as an individual remained opaque to him. He knew from the stories that Swami Sam-Kr had told him, stories that he had double-checked for himself, that Helena had been a hooker and then a junkie and that she had chosen both ways of life for herself. Master Bo-Lu suspected that part of her life had been ruled by some deep creative or destructive urge which had found no art nor science that could hold it. But this was just a guess, one among many.

Master Bo-Lu prided himself on his understanding of others, and the fact that he did not understand Helena irritated him. He could accept inscrutability and be reconciled to the mysteries within others only when they were allied to genius. And Helena did not have genius; she possessed only ingenuity. He resented her opacity, and this resentment drew his face into a scowl as he watched her. He was not aware of this until she looked at him and asked, "Whatever is the matter?"

"I beg your pardon?"

"What's wrong?"

"Nothing. Why?"

"You're looking at me as if I've offended you."

"Excuse me, but I think you are imagining things. You're overtired."

"I'm not."

"Perhaps it is my hunger then."

"Oh, I'm sorry. I forgot about lunch. I'll have something brought up right away, I am sorry." Helena reached for the telephone on her desk and, reaching for it too quickly, smacked her bandaged hand against the receiver. She bit her lip in pain. Master Bo-Lu did not seem to notice.

Of the many amazing qualities Swami Sam-Kr had once seemed to Boileau to possess, the one that had made the strongest impression upon him in the days before he became Master Bo-Lu had been Swami's way of eating. Boileau had a fairly typical North American middle-class upbringing. In his childhood, his parents had fed him the way most children of his generation had been fed: three full meals a day plus snacks between meals and special treats at bedtime. The meals themselves had always been prepared and cooked by his mother with food she had purchased sight unseen over the telephone from a grocer who had delivered them to the back door in bulging boxes two or three times a week. The meals made from these things had been simple and solid, overcooked and eaten quickly and gracelessly and thoughtlessly. He had got through meals for the sake of the dessert that always ended them and for the snacks and the treats that came later. And as he grew up, the snacks had become larger and larger and the meals shorter and shorter, until mealtime had lost its significance and he had arrived at the point where he ate whatever he wanted whenever he wanted it in whatever quantities were at hand. Any other attitude towards food had seemed to him an affectation. And then he met Swami.

Boileau's first reaction to the way in which Swami Sam-Kr ate was incredulity. The man was the slowest eater

Boileau had ever seen. He chewed every mouthful of food over and over again until it seemed to Boileau that the man must be chewing his own breath. As if this wasn't odd enough, every mouthful of food was both preceded and followed by long pauses in eating, pauses filled with comments and idle conversation. Swami talked while he ate! And before he ate and after he ate anything, he drank fruit juices sip by sip by sip. And eating and drinking so carefully, the man never ingested anything hot or cold. Everything that went into his mouth was at room temperature. Swami seemed to like that! In time, Boileau overcame incredulity and the irritation he had first felt and learned bit by bit by bit to eat in a similar manner. So it was that on this day it took Master Bo-Lu many tens of minutes to ingest the choice bits of seafood and savoury vegetables served to him. While he nibbled his food, he conversed with the two young women who had brought it to him on fine silver platters. One sat on either side of him as he reclined on pillows, and they fed him from their own hands as if he were a pasha.

The women were sisters, Nan and Fran, the newest recruits to the inner circle of The Fellowship. Master Bo-Lu recruited them himself and they were his most loyal followers, treating him with a far greater degree of respect than he ever managed to get from those whose first loyalty was to Swami. Between bites of food, he examined them on their understanding of The Rule Of The Fellowship, a document that all who wished to lead the full life of a Redeemed One had to commit to memory by order of Swami, who had devised it without the aid of a Ouija board.

"What," he began after the first bite of food crossed his lips, "are the five major offenses for which an Initiate can be expelled from The Fellowship? Tell me, Fran."

"The five major offenses for which an initiate can be expelled from The Fellowship," she began fussily, "are one, showing violence towards another initiate; two, the theft of property belonging to The Fellowship; three, practising artificial means of birth control; four, having sexual relations with one's own kind; and fifth," she hesitated a moment. "Fifth, oh I know," she continued triumphantly, "claiming mystical powers that you do not truly possess."

"Nan, has your sister spoken truly?"

"Yes, Master, except she said 'showing violence towards another member of The Fellowship.' She should have said 'displaying violence.'"

"And why is it wrong to say 'showing' rather than 'displaying'?"

"Because violence is a projection of the ego," Fran said happily.

Master Bo-Lu clapped his hands in instant applause. "Very good, Nan." He had difficulty keeping their names straight. "Now explain to me the reason why Swami through The Rule prohibits the practising of artificial means of birth control and sexual relations with one's own kind."

"Both, Master? The reasons for both?"

"Yes," he said firmly as he considered a choice prawn on the platter Fran held out to him.

"The Rule Of The Fellowship tells us that the sexual function exists not for the benefit of others but for the benefit of ourselves. It exists, The Rule tells us, in order that we may grow strong in ourselves. Thus it is that all sexual acts are good in themselves insofar as they lead to the harmonious ordering of the body. The two dangers to this proper ordering are a fear of the force of one's own fertility and, second, a fear of self-sufficiency. To relate sexually to another in perfect safety is to fall prey to both fears."

"Very good. Now, Fran, tell me . . . "

"Excuse me, Master," Nan touched him lightly on the arm, the right arm, for she always sat on his right side, even though he was not yet fully aware of that fact.

"Yes, what is it?"

"Would you explain to us once more what The Rule means by self-sufficiency and how sexual intercourse with one's own kind destroys this?"

Master Bo-Lu shifted his weight on the cushions. He liked nothing better than to answer such questions. Fran adjusted the cushions against which he leaned. He placed his hand on Nan's, stroking the tip of her smallest finger with the tip of his own finger while he sipped a long slow sip of fresh pineapple juice. When he had swallowed, he continued stroking her fingertip as he said, "Self-sufficiency. Self-sufficiency is not to be confused with egoism, which is its contrary. Egoism is the giving to the 'I' undue prominence in thought and action. Egoism is the keeping of one's thoughts upon oneself, with the constant anxious questioning of what one is thinking about oneself and what others are thinking of the oneself that thinks. It is this which leads to vanity, which is the craving for others to admire you as much as you admire yourself. It is this that destroys humility, modesty and deference. It is this that leads to ostentation. It is this that leads to exaggeration. It is this that leads to hyperbolic speaking. It is this that leads to optimism.

"And what is optimism? Optimism is the belief that everything is ordered for the best, the very best. Optimism is the doctrine that the universe is constantly tending towards a better state. This doctrine gives rise to its opposite and it is out of the opposition of things that Maya, which means 'illusion,' is created. And what is this opposite? This opposite is pessimism and the fruits of pessimism are legion: depression, mopishness, gloom, weariness, the blues, the dumps, the doldrums, the horrors, which each and severally give birth to melancholia of spirit and hypochondria of the flesh. Consider your fingertip as I stroke it with my own fingertip. Left to itself that fingertip will take what it needs from my fingertip. Left to itself that fingertip of yours will either abandon my fingertip if it does not find a strength there that it needs to perfect its own strength, or, finding a strength there that it needs to perfect its own strength, it will entwine itself with the other and follow the flowing path of energy to its root in my arm and be repulsed or attracted by the forces to be found there. But your fingertip has not been left to itself. As I stroke it, I feel within it the presence of your thoughts."

Master Bo-Lu removed his fingertip and held it at a slight distance and then with a fine deliberation of gesture removed it entirely from the area of her hand. Nan looked down at her hand. It began to quiver. To quell this, she closed her hand into a small fist.

"Open it up," he commanded her. "Lay it flat on my thigh."

She did as she was commanded.

"A little higher."

She obeyed, inching her hand up his thigh until it rested just below his scrotum.

"Leave it there," he said. "Feed me with your other hand."

As she did, she felt something stir beneath her stationary hand. She moved it a little lower down his leg.

Master Bo-Lu sighed. "The lesson is not yet learned. Return to your studies."

Nan rose sheepishly.

"Both of you," Master Bo-Lu said. "I must meditate. I advise you to do the same."

Fran rose. The two sisters gathered up the remains of the meal and made their exits with deep bows. As the door closed behind them, Master Bo-Lu drifted off to sleep.

The sleep Master Bo-Lu slept was not a passive surrender to the tiredness of his body. It was not an abdication of consciousness, a retreat into insensibility. It was more a shifting of the focus of his consciousness inwards and backwards. Something of this could be seen in the movements of his sleep. When sleep first came to him, it came as it comes to wolves and other creatures of prey. His body, once the sisters had departed, curled up into a tight ball within the surrounding cushions and the ball of his flesh hid itself beneath a light cotton coverlet. Beneath that coverlet his knees were thrust high against his breastbone, his chin thrust down to meet them. And such sleep as came to him when he was thus came in fits and starts, little naps during which the ball of his body rolled back and forth and broke wind at both ends before coming to perfect rest. Bit by bit his body uncoiled. His legs swept outwards and downwards by degrees like scissors shearing a fabric much too thick. With every movement of his legs, his head jerked upwards and his arms jerked outwards until his body was stretched out to its full extent but arched like a taut bow. Slowly, almost imperceptibly, the bow relaxed and straightened and came to rest belly-down. In this position his body breathed deeply and regularly and sonorously, toes and fingers flat and careless against the cushions.

This was the outer form of Master Bo-Lu's body in sleep.

Inwardly, his consciousness shifted and moved in as many ways. In curling up into a ball, Master Bo-Lu sloughed off his identity as Master Of The Fellowship Of Maya Redeemers and became Adrian (Bolo) Boileau once more. As Bolo Boileau, he fell into the sleep of a taxi driver, of a man of the streets who was smart and careful, self-protective, alert to the dangers of his environment, jealous and guarded in his territory. Fears beset him. He was afraid of fire and his nose sniffed for smoke. He was afraid of intruders and his ears pricked at every small noise in the building. Then when his nose and ears were satisfied, these primal fears retreated and gave way to the thoughts and the worries that joined him to the everyday world, the world in which automobiles had accidents and required repairs, a world of streets and traffic signs and patrol cars and private cars and buses and trucks and other taxis, a world of skilled and unskilled drivers and careless pedestrians. Bolo Boileau loved and hated that world in equal measure. The things that he loved about it and the things he hated about it, the things that he relished and the things that he despised were all jumbled together when he was awake to that world.

But in sleep they disengaged from one another, fell into patterns of pleasure and pain. He rolled one way with the pain that came from the sudden swerves, the quick brakings of the actual driving. He rolled another way with the curses and cursing that punctuated the driving. He rolled with the pleasures he took in getting the better of other drivers. And rolling this way and that, he recapitulated his night as a taxi driver. And, rocked by the alternating currents of pleasure and pain, he was lulled and lulled until his whole lower being relaxed and released the tensions that had gripped it. And the tensions passed out of him in burps and farts.

Bolo Boileau's body at rest disconnected itself from the everyday world. The currents of pleasure and pain were swept upwards into his head and transmitted into pictures, into elemental images of his day. As each picture composed itself, some power within him froze it and framed it and hung it within the gallery that was his memory. It was this hanging of mental canvasses that uncoiled him and stretched him into a taut bow. It was in this position that he roamed through those galleries and fashioned the static pictures into a film, a dream. He dreamed that he was on a beach among a group of young men playing volleyball. He saw himself watch the ball sail over the net and fall at his feet. He kicked it, and in kicking it he saw that it was not a ball at all but a severed head. He saw himself pick up this severed head and look at it. It was the head of Swami Sam-Kr. He laced it over his own head as if it were a rubber mask. As he did this, he felt a change come over him.

He stood in a grassy field enclosed within an old-fashioned schoolroom with high green walls and many windows. The windows were covered with blackout curtains and the whole room was lit by a single bulb. The young men of the beach had turned into wizened old men in soutanes and he recognized the faces of the priests who had taught him in the seminary. But he was no longer himself. The severed head had transformed him into Swami Sam-Kr and the priests were full of indignation at the sight. Ranged across the opposite end of the field, they formed a choir that chanted "Whore-monger, whore-monger" at him in Gregorian tones. The field was suddenly divided by a volleyball net but this net was in fact a spider-web, and the spider that had woven it, a gigantic black beast with the face of Helena, hung at its very centre and leered at him. The she-spider opened her mouth and a snake uncoiled and uncoiled until its head reached his genitals and began to perform fellatio on him. The eldest of the priests served a great black ball and smashed it at him. As it touched his hands the ball turned into a book. Back and forth the book bounced as he ran faster and faster to keep up the pace set by the ancient priests, who moved back and forth across the court like black birds. Finally he won the right to serve, but the book hit the net and was consumed by the great she-spider. Each of the black birds spat new books out of their mouths and put them into play against him. He grew frantic, lashed out wildly. The books turned into young men and were swallowed whole by the she-spider.

Among their number, he saw himself — Bolo Boileau — swallowed by the snake within the she-spider's mouth. He saw himself fall from a great height and land upside down in his taxi. His feet steered. His hands worked the pedals. The car sped blindly into a wall. He saw himself right side up try to reverse the car, but the wall became a dragon and he drove into its mouth. He was being swallowed whole, cut off from world and air. Then, out of nowhere, the severed head of Swami Sam-Kr rose up in the dragon's throat and barred his further fall while a hand grabbed his leg from above and pulled him out. He woke up. And, awakening, he found himself truly awake and lying on his bed of cushions; a small hand was stroking his thigh. He lifted his head and saw Nan kneeling beside him.

"I am here for another lesson, Master," she said timidly. "Would you demonstrate the meaning of self-sufficiency once more?"

He did not quite feel up to it but he did his best. It was better than going back to sleep and discovering the end of his dream.

JE T'AIME, COWBOY

Even though Perrault speaks serviceable English, the term *garage sale* confuses him. These two words put together in this way always suggest to him that it is *le garage* itself that is for sale. But that is only a momentary thing, good for a quick laugh at his own expense. There is another, deeper confusion that registers within him when he sees these words — the confusion of a man suddenly caught out of his depth. Garage sales are an *anglais* thing. People in his own parish of St-Henri never sell the things they no longer use. What they don't need, they give away. If one does not have a poor relation or neighbour, there is always the parish church with its clothing and furniture collection for fire victims. The only things that aren't needed are the things nobody could ever use — refrigerators stripped of motors and autos stripped of every possible part that are as burnt-out and skeletal as the gutted houses in whose yards they squat. And so Perrault always accelerates when he passes a Garage Sale: they are foreign, incomprehensible. More, they are somehow indecent. Thus it is that he responds with great misgiving when an English woman in a halter and very short shorts absolutely insists that he stop and look at the things she has for sale. But there is no getting out of it: she corners him when he makes his delivery next door and grabs hold of his arm and steers him into her yard.

He looks around wildly, dazzled by the closeness of the woman, the touch of her fingers on his arm, the richness of her surroundings. Her house is long, white and low with an attached double garage in the best part of Beaconsfield. Two cars sit in her driveway — a little Honda Civic and a large black BMW sedan. Both are nearly new. At the sight of them, Perrault draws away from the woman's touch. Cars are one of the great passions of his life. Neither of these are kinds that he has ever dreamed of owning but the BMW is a mechanical beauty and wonderfully engineered. He lets his fingertips float over its fine lines. He stares through its windows and whistles at the array of instruments. Then he catches sight of the woman's reflection in the window. Women are another of the passions of his life. But not this one. She is small, lean and shrivelled-up looking. The grey-black fringe of her bobbed hair comes down over her brows. Her face is sun-weathered, sunken-cheeked. There are deep brackets around her mouth. Her lips are hard. Her brows arch automatically. She has rounded, sloped shoulders and a heavily freckled body. Her yellow halter seems quite empty, flat.

"I'm selling it too," she says.

"How much?" The question is automatic.

"Oh, I don't know . . . . I hadn't really thought about it until just now . . . . It's a model 603i, isn't it? Why don't we say six hundred and thirty dollars."

"Six hundred thirty dollars!" Perrault whistles. The BMW is worth maybe eighteen, maybe twenty thousand. But it doesn't matter to him. Her simple-minded ridiculous price is still five hundred dollars more than he can pay. He says nothing. There is no need to say anything. Either the car or the woman is missing a gear or two. He bets it is the woman.

Her hand grasps his elbow. He feels himself being steered beyond the cars and into the shadow of the garage. He moves slowly and carefully around a golf cart and clubs. Inside the doorway, there are all sorts of things arranged haphazardly on a couple of garden tables and along a chrome coat rack — sports clothing and sports equipment. The clothing doesn't interest him at all. But he is drawn to the tennis and other racquets, the fly rods, spinning reels, boxes of lures and flies, the rifles, scopes, target pistols, the skis and the skates, the sticks and the pads. All of it is as good as new. It occurs to him suddenly that it might all be stolen. *Mais c'est pas possible.* This lady is just a little deranged but her man, he must really be crazy: nobody can use this stuff up in two long lifetimes.

"How about this?" The woman directs his gaze to a leather case with brass fittings. She unlatches it. Inside, fitted into the kind of green felt they use on billiards tables, is a double-barrelled shotgun. A very fine one. He knows only a little bit about guns but he can see that this is one of the best. It's an Orvis. It has a ventilated rib and a single trigger and a beavertail forearm. The stock is walnut. He cannot resist taking it from the case and fitting it together and trying it against his own shoulder. But it is too big. He can hardly reach the trigger. Damn, it is a real beauty. He holds it in front of him. He notices that the stock is inlaid with gold in the form of initials. H.P.P. At a certain angle, the flowing ornate lines of the H can almost be read as a J. J.P.P. — his own initials: Jean Paul Perrault. "How much?"

"What gauge is it?"

"A twelve."

"It has two barrels, hasn't it? It'll cost you twenty-four bucks."

If she is crazy, she is crazy. He takes a twenty-dollar bill out of his wallet. So much for his savings. He takes four ones from his trouser pocket. So much for his beer money.

The money is nothing to her. She hardly looks at it before thrusting it carelessly into the top of her halter. She leaves it and herself a bit exposed. The money is more seductive than her breasts. "Do you want to know why I am doing this?"

He says nothing. He begins taking the gun apart and putting it back inside its case — his gun, his case.

"I'll tell you why I am doing this. The shithead who

owns all this stuff — my husband — is in Mexico with his secretary. That's why I'm doing all this. He left me three weeks ago. He says it's business. I know his kind of business. Monkey business. Then she phones me. He's been busted by the Mexican police. He needs money. So she says. Tough shit. Everything's in my name, everything that counts. He's got the car and this shit. She phones again. He really needs money. He can have money, I tell her. He can have what I get for his stuff. You've fucked him for twenty-four bucks. You can fuck me for free."

Perrault keeps his eyes on the table. He sees a small pistol. He picks it up.

"Get the hell out of here," she says. "Go. Get lost, creep."

He goes. He doesn't notice that he still has her handgun until he gets in his truck. Then he is too nervous to go back and confront her craziness again. He jams the pistol into his pocket.

When he finishes his deliveries, Perrault goes back to the depot and slips his guns into his own car. It takes a little doing. The boss keeps a sharp eye on his drivers. The boss is *un vrai Pepsi* — empty from the shoulders up. Nobody steals anything from the delivery trucks. It's too risky. You want something from the store, you go through the shipping clerk. Marcel knows the angles. Marcel is *un vrai chum*. He punches out and then waits for Marcel. He has promised him a ride home. Marcel is his chum.

Perrault's car doesn't stop at the depot gate.

"The brakes, they should be fixed," Marcel says.

"I know, I know. One hundred forty dollars they want. I got a hundred. Another two weeks, maybe. That's if Monique doesn't need anything extra; that's if the kid doesn't need anything extra."

"You should sell this wreck."

"And buy what? A Stingray? Twenty bucks down, twenty bucks a week. For sure. They give them away to guys like me."

"This and three hundred could get you something better. I know this guy."

"You always know a guy, Marcel, but the guys you know, I don't want to know. Me, now I know this woman. You get us six hundred dollars and she'll have us driving a BMW."

"What?"

Perrault tells him about the crazy lady and her garage sale. He tries to draw back before he comes to the part about the guns, but it just slips out. He curses himself. Marcel is not a man who should be told about guns. Having been told about them, he has to see them. Right away. Perrault pulls into a side street beside a factory.

"I can get you two, maybe even three hundred dollars for these. I know this guy."

"I don't want to sell them."

"But you say the shotgun is too big for you."

"I can have it cut down."

"Yeah, okay. For sure. I know you want to be the classiest rat hunter in the parish. But you better get rid of that pistol. The cops catch you with it, they might not understand. Your wife, the same thing. But look, I do know this guy. He does nice work. He'll fix the shotgun for you. He'll take the pistol and give you enough money for new brakes. You better think about it. It's my life too you've got to think about. You think hard about it."

Perrault thinks about nothing else all evening. Monique and the kid are downstairs at her mother's. There is just the television set for company. Everything he looks at is either men and women arguing or cops chasing people. He can't tell Monique about the guns. She would just hate them. She just wouldn't see the point of his buying the shotgun. It would just frighten her. It is no good even trying to explain to her that he has bought it, not because it is a gun but because it is something beautiful and well-made, something better than he has ever hoped to own. Something that is first class. But if he tries to get rid of them, what will happen?

Marcel's friend has his shop in a little shopping plaza over in Laval. They drive over there on their next day off.

But Monique insists on coming along and bringing the kid with her. They have told her some fine story about going to get a part for Marcel's auto, the one that never works. And he has the guns wrapped up in an old coat as if they were just some greasy auto parts. But there is no place to park near the shop. He and Marcel have to cross the parking lot with the guns. Some old codger sees them and thinks that they are going to rob somebody. The old guy calls the cops. He's just pocketing the money when the door flies open and his kid comes rushing right in and starts blubbering that Monique has gone into labour. They run back to the car and speed off to the hospital and some drunk of a cop plays cowboy and tries to run them into the ground and his brakes fail and they are all killed. That's what happens. For sure. He can just see it happening to him. He turns off the television set.

He has hidden his guns at the very back of the kitchen pantry in the big bin where he stores the spare parts he likes to salvage from other people's wrecks. He takes them out. He assembles the shotgun. It really is far too big for him. It is engraved with the wrong initials. The H just isn't a J. Even so, it is so very beautiful, so very fine that he knows he cannot part with it. He buries it deeper in his hidey hole. It is the most beautiful thing he will ever own. He takes the pistol and stuffs it in the pocket of an old jacket that has been put aside with some other things for the next parish clothing drive. It will be a big joke on the priest. He puts the coffee on. He waits for Monique. He waits for his daughter.

When he climbs into bed after his bath, his wife snuggles her backside up to him until they lie as close together as spoons in a drawer. He pats her on the belly. "I have a name for our son," he says. "We will call him Henri, my pet. Henri Paul Perrault. We are going to make him big and strong and give him beautiful things. He is going to be a fine rich man. He'll even have his own country place. In the autumn, he is going to shoot ducks for sport. Just like the Americans. He is going to be so big and so beautiful, he's not going to have to take shit from anybody. But it will be good for such a man to remember where he came from. It is no bad thing to be named after the saint of the parish in which you are born."

Monique says nothing. She understands his mood. He is always like this, always so full of plans for his unborn son when he has had a bad day with the English ladies. If she stays quiet, says nothing at all, he will tell her the whole story. He is so unlike other men, he keeps nothing to himself. He has no secrets. Even the mystery of his autos, he keeps in her kitchen. She will have to do something about that. It is unhealthy. Maybe tomorrow, she will have her father make room for those things in his shed. But she puts the thought aside. Her husband is telling his story. She does not want to miss a word. She wants to know exactly how it is that his wallet is missing a twenty-dollar bill. He is so unlike other men that he does not even hide his wallet when he takes a bath. But that is good. She always knows — without asking — how things stand between them and the world. When he finishes his story, she will let him ride her from behind. When he bucks and roars, she will whisper, *Je t'aime, Cowboy*.

BETTER DAYS

"You've got to be eighteen. Minimum, by law."

"I am eighteen."

"Really?"

"Really!"

To Dieter, she looks fourteen going on forty. Maybe it's the lights, maybe it's the time of the day, maybe it's just her foreign features. "What's your birth date?"

"June twenty-first, 1972."

"At least you've rehearsed. I get a lot of girls who don't know when they were born."

"This is my driver's licence. This is my social insurance card."

Dieter stares at plastic rectangles, fingers them. "What did you say your name was?"

"I said Nana."

"These say Nanette."

"So, it's Nanette. Nanette Nhon, born Saigon, June twenty-first, 1972. Really."

"Well, Miss Nhon from Saigon, you'd better fill in a form. Sit down. Here's a pen. Want a drink?"

"Vodka. A shooter, please."

Eighteen. Really. When he was eighteen, clubs were off-limits. The legal drinking age was twenty-one and he'd done most of his drinking in the back seats of parked cars. Beer. But that was '62. *Happy Days!* Bullshit. Hollywood puts a nice a gloss on things. Le Java Hava Drive-In, the place where kids had hung out and done their drinking in his home town across the river in the Townships, would never have made it into the movies. No gloss. Le Java Hava was a big piece of asphalt by the side of the road — a parking apron designed to hold a dozen semitrailers, but the trucks only stopped in the mornings and by night it was big and dark enough to hold all the hot rods in town. Le Java Hava Drive-In was a big neon sign on a small cinder-block building tacked on to the side of a no-name service station that did custom work for rodders.

"I'll go fill this out over there on stage, okay boss?"

Dieter shrugs and hands her the shot glass of vodka and Nana Nhon wanders over to the empty stage and fiddles with the lights. She hums as she adjusts a white spotlight to her liking so that it illuminates her as she sits down at the piano. She picks out a tune he doesn't recognize. But he recognizes the move: she's going to audition for him whether he likes it or not. They'll say anything to get their foot in the front door, all these waitresses who want to be singers. But it could be worse. It could be the seventies again and he could be running a disco and the girls could be dancers and everybody could be doing cocaine.

Le Java Hava, he suddenly remembers, was an L-shaped counter with stools and four cramped booths that could hold six midgets, four normal adults or two truckers and their idea of a breakfast. It was a cigarette machine and a juke box and a couple of coolers wedged into the corners, plates and dusty glassware and a lot of hand-painted signs advertising the stuff that got served. There were pictures on the walls — basic low-rent ain't-nature-wonderful calender scenes in plastic-made-to-look-like-wood frames. Le Java Hava was a short order grill and a deep fryer, a stove, a walk-in cooler, a soft ice cream machine, a couple of big coffee urns, a soda dispenser, a big sink and as many shelves as the walls could support. The shelves were piled to tumbling-down point with disposable plates and cups and wrappers of a dozen different kinds and big yellow jars of mustard, big green jars of sweet pickle relish, big red jars of ketchup. Not Heinz. An opening had been let into the outside wall and was equipped with a sliding window so trays could be passed from the kitchen to the parking lot. Le Java Hava was where he worked when he was sixteen pretending to be eighteen.

Nana Nhon stops doodling at the piano, starts filling in the application form. Dieter watches her tap the end of the pen against her red lips. Good lips. Thick, juicy, pouting Mitsou lips. If she can carry a tray of drinks, maybe they can find some waitressing hours for her. His throat is dry. He pulls himself a half-pint of Double D from the pump.

Summer '60 was hot, dry and full of failing crops, empty cows, skinny sheep. People stopped spending money. He had a job in a Township department store selling men's white shirts, ties and good old reliable English-worsted charcoal-grey-flannel going-to-church suits. But nobody was buying. The store manager told him he was laid off. He knew he was fired. When he picked up his pay, the bookkeeper told him that she knew Le Java Hava needed a cashier.

There was a sign hanging on the front door: Reliable Cashier Wanted. He took down the sign, screwed up his courage, flung open the door, ambled over to the girl behind the counter, said, "I'm your man."

"Not unless you've got at least eight thick inches," she said.

What could he say? He was from the right side of town and she wasn't. So he blushed and flashed the sign from the door and told her he wanted the job. He stammered badly.

She arched a pencilled-in brow and bawled back over her shoulder, "Georges, a D-d-d-d-d-dieter to see you."

Georges had been a professional midget wrestler. He was barely four feet tall and a lizard: greased hair, thin moustache, tight silk suit, lots of gold jewelry on a compact muscular body with a full-size head. Georges tested his arithmetic and his French.

"You're one of the Hungarian refugee kids, aren't you?"

"That's right."

"Me, I'm not prejudiced. Stick around and you can start right in on the four o'clock shift."

"What do I make?"

"Any trouble and you're out of here. Hey, laugh, kid — that was a joke. The minimum for a week and then we'll see if you're worth more. And kid, keep the shirt and tie. It's got class. Maybe some other people will take the hint."

When Georges explained the job to him, it seemed very easy. All he had to do was take bills from carhops out back and the waitress in front, check sums, collect money, make change carefully. At the end of his eight-hour shift he counted the takings and tallied it against the receipts and put it in a blue canvas bag and handed it to Georges. But the job wasn't nearly as simple as it first seemed. Once he started, he had to work fast. Business came in waves. Drenched and dripping exhaustion from every pore, he discovered that he was thirty dollars short on the first night's takings. He had no idea what had happened.

But Georges said, "Good work, kid, you're already cutting my losses. Usually the girls take forty a night. A couple more days and they won't get anything past you. There's a raise for you as soon as you get it coming out right. And I'll give you an extra fifty as soon as you show me which girl is the ringleader. Who do you think it is?"

He had no idea. All the carhops looked equally villainous. But he was willing to play detective — he needed the raise and wanted the bonus.

"I can wait on tables. I can tend bar too. Really. I'm a good artist if you need signs — French and English," she says as she hands in the application form.

Nana Nhon's handwriting is full of flourishes, artistic,

difficult for him to read. "Mix me a drink, Nana Nhon. Mix me a Bloody Mary."

He watches the girl who wants to be a waitress until she can be a singer move behind the bar and pour three fingers of vodka and six fingers of tomato juice. He watches her add a teaspoon of lemon, a teaspoon of Worcestershire, two drops of tabasco, three pinches of salt — sea, celery and garlic — and serve it to him on a napkin. They can't have her work the bar, she's too short.

"Cheers."
"Is it good?"
"Terrific. Are you eighteen? Really."
"Really! June twenty-first, 1972."
"When did you get out of Viet Nam?"
"I'm not a boat person. I was an Embassy baby. 1973."
"You were raised in the States?"
"New Jersey. My parents split up. I live with my aunt. Do I get a job?"
"Do you have Landed Immigrant status?"
"I have a student visa."
"Take a look around the place. See where things are."

It took a week to put an end to obvious thefts but it took him a few days more to realize what honesty was costing him. Georges couldn't remember anything about having promised him a raise. The carhops made mistakes with the orders so that good food was wasted. Or it would have gone to waste if he hadn't let the girls eat it without paying for it. Then the girls started taking it for granted that he'd do whatever work they left undone. And he did because whenever he stood on his dignity, they just started talking dirty.

A lot of different girls worked at Le Java Hava Drive-In but French or English, they were all more or less the same — crude, dumb and not pretty — except Cerise, who was really vulgar, stupid, whorish. The other girls did everything but "go all the way" with just about any guy who came their way. Not Cerise. She liked to brag about being "orgied" by four or six guys at a time on the livingroom carpet in the middle of the afternoon while her mom was gutting chickens at the poultry plant. And Cerise liked to tell the other carhops — right in front of him — that he was about the only person in the world that she wouldn't give head. She called him *Le Squarehead*. Then he caught her trying to take money from the cash register. Georges took her for a ride in his Cadillac and they both came back smiling. He didn't get his bonus and Cerise didn't get fired.

One night Cerise came running up to the take-out window looking like she'd been pulled through a hedge backwards.

"Some guys just tried to rape me."

"Who?"

"Those guys in the Merc!"

He looked out over the lot. There was a louvred and lowered metallic purple '51 Mercury at the far end. He laughed.

"What's wrong with them? Too nice for you?"

She let fly with a whole tray of half-eaten food.

He had soggy french fries in his hair, mustard and relish on his eyeglasses, hamburger meat up his nose, cold chicken gravy running down his chin, bits of lettuce and onions sticking to his teeth, and his shirt was plastered with bread crusts and chicken bones. And Cerise was screaming.

Under the spotlight over by the piano, Nana Nhon has the look all this year's crop of girl singers are copying. She's wearing black and silver cowboy boots and black tights and a little black skirt that barely covers her bum and a silver ornamented belt and a black lace camisole. The oversize black jacket she had been wearing is slung casually over a chair as she sits at the piano and begins playing and singing Bruce Springsteen's song about a lost soul on the New Jersey Turnpike. Her voice is as wasted as a junkie's, a Cowboy Junkie's. She's been listening to Margot Timmins. Dieter tries to gauge her crowd appeal. A lot of the regulars, women and men, he guesses, will be devastated by her Asian-American streetwalker bad girl good looks and her waif manner.

When Nana Nhon finishes her song, she smiles and looks at him too expectantly.

"Can you do something upbeat for me?"

"Like what?"

"What about Springsteen's 'Pink Cadillac'?"

"I don't think I know it."

"Of course you know it. The one on the radio all the time, the one Natalie Cole sings." He sings the opening phrase.

"Teach it to me! I learn fast. I've got to go take a pee, then I'll do it with you, okay?"

Cerise's brother pulled up in a '34 Ford dragster, heard her story, went wild. He was going to kill all the guys in the '51 Merc. Dieter had better come along and help him do it. It was a set-up and Cerise's brother helped them thump him around. They formed lines about four feet apart and pushed him from one side to the other. They kept their knees up and bashed him back and front and chopped at him with their arms as they called him *tête carré, bohunk, Bosché, Nazi, Commie, bâtard*. Cerise's brother set up like a boxer and when Dieter got shoved at him, he hauled back and threw a punch that sent eyeglasses flying and nose moving sideways and teeth rattling and blood gushing.

Cerise's brother dragged him back to the restaurant and told everybody that Dieter was some sort of hero and that the gang in the '51 Merc had gotten the worst of it. He couldn't speak because of the bleeding. He just let Georges drive him to the hospital where a doctor stitched up his cheek and straightened his nose and gave him some painkillers. Georges waited and drove him home.

As he stepped out of the Cadillac, Georges told him, "If you've got to fight, use your knees and feet and arms and bite if you have to, but fists are stupid, a *maudit Anglais* game. There's no way you can keep working where people can see your face. But I won't fire you this time. You'll learn. I got another job you can do, a downtown job. We'll talk tomorrow."

They sat together in the tiny office at the back of a town restaurant and Georges showed him all the fine stuff that the Chicken Delight people had sent him. Georges had decided to go into the southern fried chicken business. It was going to make him a millionaire. All you had to do was to get people to eat it once and they'd be addicted. They'd never buy the Colonel's stuff again.

But how did you get people to try something new? By giving them a free sample. And how did you do that? You build a great big papier-mâché chicken head just like the one on the Chicken Delight logo. You put a chef's hat on it. You put the whole apparatus on the shoulders of a guy with sandwich boards flapping back and front announcing this newest food sensation. You stuff a big bunch of balloons in one hand and free dinner vouchers in the other and put him downtown.

Dieter walked the streets. The wind blew his chicken head this way and that. The sandwich boards banged the hell out of his knees. Little kids screamed at the sight of him. Bigger kids kicked him in the shins when he refused to give them seconds. And Cerise's brother and his friends in the purple '51 Merc cruised along behind him calling out, "Eh chickenshit, chickenshit, poulet-poo, your cock does doodle-doo."

He quit after two days. Georges wasn't happy with him. But the ex-wrestler wasn't a man to hold a grudge. Georges gave him another job at Le Java Hava Drive-In.

Better Days

Up at the piano, he hunts out chords, finds the melody, sings the opening verse to "Pink Cadillac." Nana Nhon catches hold of the tune and hums along, tries out a couple of harmonic flourishes and gets them almost right. Dieter likes the way she slips right into the rhythm. He beckons her to the piano bench.

"I liked the way you joined in without knowing the words," he says as she swings herself up on the bench beside him, bumps hips. "You sure you don't already know this?"

"I don't. Not really!"

"Yeah, okay, then, let's do it. It's a favourite of my partner."

"Really!"

"Yeah. Springsteen came into this club once. After a concert."

"What was he like?"

"Nobody believed it was him."

"Really!"

"Really. You're eighteen?"

"June twenty-first, 1972. I'll do anything for a job. Really."

"Okay, sing."

For the rest of the summer he washed pots and pans, carried out slops, scrubbed floors and found himself a whole lot happier than he'd ever been before. He became nearly invisible in his splattered white pants and T-shirt. He observed people without being observed. He got to know their weaknesses. With Cerise, it was a diamond ring.

One day when he was sweeping off the parking lot, he found an engagement ring. He figured it was just paste but that didn't matter. He took a knife and loosened the stone. He took it back to the kitchen and showed it around. Cerise was dumping rancid beef patties in the garbage. She really wanted to try the ring on. He let her but as he slipped it over her knuckle, the diamond fell into the refuse container.

"It's yours if you can find it," he said.

He waited until she had soggy french fries in her hair, mustard and relish on her cheeks, hamburger meat up her nose, cold chicken gravy running down her chin, bits of lettuce and onions sticking to her teeth, and until her blouse was plastered with bread crusts and chicken bones and the floor of the kitchen was ankle deep in trash. Then he showed her the diamond, which had fallen all the way into his other hand. It was a genuine diamond. He bought a ticket to Montreal and swapped the jewel for a Gibson guitar he still has hanging on his livingroom wall.

"I think we might be able to find something for you to do around here but it's my partner who takes care of the hiring. I do the firing. You'll have to talk to him."

"Do you think he'll like me?" she asks and leans over the piano. Her camisole falls forward and there is enough light for him to see her breasts, small perfect breasts, distinct from her torso with deep brown conical nipples. He knows that if it was the seventies still and she was a dancer and he had cocaine up his nose, he would probably reach up her skirt and she'd probably open her legs wide and welcome his fingers. The pantihose always came off when the dancer went for the pee. Disco days. Disco daze.

"The man has a wicked sense of humour. He's sort of like a full size Danny DeVito. Sing 'Pink Cadillac' for him. Wiggle your ass a bit. He'll like that. And Nana Nhon, you don't have to put out for him. Or me. Come back in a couple of hours. Ask for Jean Jacques."

"Really. But you don't like me? You don't like Oriental girls. I like you."

"You sing it solo this time."

Eighteen. '62. Nineteen. Twenty. His first hitch in the US Army. Twenty-one. Re-enlistment. Viet Nam. Saigon. Doll-like girls wrapped up skintight in china silk red dresses with slits up the sides that didn't stop where their legs did, a special girl with big Mitsou lips and high heels as red as her dress and Bette Davis eyes.

The first time he saw her he thought he'd stepped right into one of the trashy detective novels where women who looked like that always got a bullet in the breast.

The last time he had seen her, she had rice in her hair, shellfish up her nose, a black fluid like soya sauce running down her chin, bits of silk and skin sticking to her teeth and her dress was plastered with broken bones and blood. The floor of the comfort house was ankle deep in offal and the smell of cordite was heavy on the air and he was screaming and missing something he never got back. Innocence.

Nana Nhon is getting the hang of her new song. She is very happy, very excited. She thinks she has had an audition, gotten a break. She doesn't quite understand that he doesn't need any pleasing, that his end of the business is to be tough, get rid of people.

Once Nana Nhon has gone, Dieter will get back to what he was doing when she came in. He's trying to figure out who is shorting them at the till. He's trying to figure out who he can fire, who the other guy hasn't already taken for a ride.

A HOLE WITH A HEAD IN IT

A tape is playing. An acoustic guitar, string bass and dobro plaintively accompany a strong male voice, a voice that can be believed when it sings of a river of tears flowing through all lives. It is a voice Butch wishes he had inside his own head. It is the voice of a man who has come to terms with all of love's potions and poisons. Butch drinks in the words and repeats them to himself and the tape keeps rolling and another song unfolds and passes by, scarcely heard, and then this stranger's advice to a too-faithful friend to shake himself loose of a bad companion gets inside his head and he stops merely listening and starts living the lyrics and remembering things he would rather forget. And Butch shakes his head. It is a voluntary movement. He tells himself he is some kind of an idiot. And the shaking moves involuntarily from his head through his neck and down his spine as a shiver, spreading through his ribcage and hitting his heart like a hammer blow, and his arms tremble and his knees go weak. And Butch tells himself it is only tiredness, not illness. He is not sick. He is not going to get sick. He is not going to develop pneumonia. Or anything else. The only illness he suffers from is a kind of sickness of the head: he is a dunderhead, a fool, an idiot. He tells himself that he is some kind of an idiot. He tells himself that he is some kind of idiot to have come back to Montreal simply because Florio is sick and said he needed him. He tells himself that he is a fool for love. He tells himself that he is a fool for loving Florio the way he does. He tells himself things he has told himself a hundred thousand times since he arrived in Montreal at Florio's loft on The Main. A million times. A million million times since he has known Florio.

But they do no good, no good at all: his curses and imprecations against Florio's hold on him are as useless as the prayers he used to say over and over again when he was a good little Catholic boarding school boy trying to shake himself free from the filthy sinful habits his flesh was so prone to indulge in under the covers late at night in the dormitory. Prayers. Hymns. He had hated praying. It had never done him any good. He had enjoyed masturbating far too much! But he had liked the hymns, he had liked singing. He had used the liturgical music to shut out the sense of sinfulness in his flesh. He wishes he could use this music to shut out the words Florio inspires inside his head but the sentiments are too close to the bone. He needs music that he has heard a thousand times or more. He needs sentimental lyrics that will hug his skin like shrink wrap around a record album. He needs the kind of songs he sings and plays when he gigs at piano bars for lovers who need consoling. He needs the kind of music he was making for suburbanites out on the town in Kingston when he heard of Florio's illness and came running up to Montreal, leaving broken hearts and a broken contract behind him. But Florio doesn't have any Tin Pan Alley songs around the flat any more. All his old albums, all the music Butch once shared with him is gone now and in its place are stacks of cassettes filled with the songs of singers he does not know. Like this one by T Bone Burnett.

T Bone Burnett's *T Bone Burnett* drew him first by the shadowy John Lennon face on the cover and then by Tom Waits's "Time" on the second side. Butch has been teaching himself some Tom Waits tunes and routines to lift his act a little from the doldrums into which it has descended in recent years, years that have found him more often gigging the piano bars of towns like Kingston and Cornwall and Peterborough than playing Toronto and Montreal, where he began when his talent was fresher and his looks were better.

A Hole With A Head In It

T Bone Burnett. There is a hush to this tape that feels like being alone in a church, in a school chapel, in childhood. But oh, the words, the words are caustic with truths that keen in his head like banshees, witches, mothers. Mothers. Mummies. Butch tries hard not to think of his mother and what his mother will say when she hears that he has been in Montreal with Florio again. *After all this time! After all these years,* he can hear Mummy begin, *you're still an idiot, dear, when it comes to that man. He's too flighty for you. He can't ever settle down to anything or anyone, now can he? Why do you want to waste yourself in a meaningless relationship?* And what will he say in reply? He can say that yes, he is an idiot. But he cannot say this to Mummy. He can say this only to himself. And to Florio. And only to Florio when Florio cannot hear him. He hopes that Florio can hear the music playing on the stereo. Butch wants him to hear T Bone Burnett sing about *meaningless, poisonous* words of love.

Butch wants Florio to wake up and tell him that this time everything is different, this time he can have all the love that Florio has it in himself to give, that this time it is love forever and ever, amen. But this is a futile wish, a wish as futile as a child's prayer. Florio cannot answer any prayers. He is too sick, too drugged with antibiotics and painkillers, too pneumonic. Butch is alone and cold and shaking. Shaken. He should get up and turn up the heat against the damp chill of late November but all he can do is sit and rock in his chair and listen to this unsentimental, caustic music of love gone wrong and try not to think too much of his mother's reactions.

Florio. Flow rio. The river that was and is Florio began forty years ago in southwestern Saskatchewan as Floyd Keller Junior in a small hospital in a small town on a clay-white river in Cypress Hills country within sight of an oil derrick his father had rigged. It was a dry well but a sticky, wet, messy premature son that the Kellers brought into the world. Later, Mr. Keller would have good luck with oil and bad luck with his son but at birth Floyd Junior was the fulfilment of a dream that went deeper into a father's heart than black gold. Butch knows this to be true. He has heard this story from Florio's father and he has believed it and has had his belief confirmed by photographs of the father with his infant son. It is one of the very few stories he has heard that he has ever believed about Florio's childhood. Still, he knows in general terms what that childhood must have been like. It cannot be that dissimilar from his own. He and Florio have long been two of a kind, sensitive prairie boys of artistic temperament, crybabies, sickly sorts. Butch grew up hating his weakness and despising his cowardice and trying to pretend that neither existed. But they existed, how they existed! In the womanish world that he had inhabited, the pretence had worked tolerably well. In Florio's more mannish world, a sorry history of self-contempt cut deeper and consequently was denied more forcibly. The crude folk culture of oil towns and cattle lands had made Florio mouthy, a tall-tale-teller, a congenital liar, a truly maddening man.

Rocking back and forth, Butch tries to keep time with the easy light swing of T Bone Burnett's country tunes played on acoustic instruments. But it doesn't quite work because the music has subtleties that get lost in Butch's anger and resentments against Florio, against himself. Losing patience with himself and with the cowboy musician, he turns his chair a quarter turn so that he can see the face of Florio's long-case clock and rock to the steadier rhythms of its pendulum. It is a pretty clock with an easy beat and it holds good memories for him. It was the first really fine present he'd bought for Florio when they first lived together. The clock had been broken but was still valuable and he had fixed it and made it as priceless as their love and friendship had been in those far-off days. Later, when things had soured a little, he had been glad to leave it behind — a parting gift. Butch watches time pass over the ornate face of the antique clock. He watches its golden sun set and its silver moon rise mechanically and he looks out the window and sees that yes, it is evening now, and he thinks that yes, it is evening in more senses than one. Everything in the world he has known and loved best is aging, shrivelling, dying stupidly, idiotically. Again and again, rocking back and forth, back and forth, Butch tells himself that he must get out of the chair, must do something. What? Do what? He could tidy the studio. He could set Florio's encrusted brushes to soak in tins of fresh solvent. He could turn some of Florio's more recent paintings, the ones that most disturb him, the ones that are too terribly chic, the ones that the Yuppie dealers fight to hang, the ones that are quite dead, to the wall. To do this would be to subtract something from Florio and to add something to himself, to assert that he has preserved standards that Florio has glibly tossed aside. But Butch doesn't have the energy to make such a statement. He has hardly enough energy to make a cup of tea but he is dreadfully thirsty so he does get out of his chair and says, "Yes, I must make some tea. I'm not coming down with anything. I just need to warm up a little."

2

Butch makes tea the way his mother taught him to make tea years and years ago, lifetimes ago. He now makes tea the way tea was always made for the ladies who came to play bridge and talk across the card tables in the front parlour of the big brick house on the Crescents in Regina, Saskatchewan, that was his family's home. It is the way Butch has always made tea for his lovers. It is made by warming a silver teapot upside down over the jet of steam rising from a kettle of fresh water that has just begun to boil. It is made by spreading loose English Breakfast tea leaves across the bottom of the pot before adding boiling water. It is made by gently steeping the tea leaves for precisely six minutes — six minutes measured off by the grains of sand in an egg timer, twice upended. It is made by pouring the tea through a stainless steel strainer into milk that has already been poured into the bottom of a bone china cup. Florio's teapot needs polishing, the grains of sand are sticky in the timer, the strainer has stains, none of the cups any longer has a matching saucer. Butch closes his eyes to these details. He stands at a sink full of dirty dishes and drinks his tea quickly. He wants instant energy. He wants to do something. He knows he ought to do some housework. He pours himself a second cup of tea. He leans against the counter. He closes his eyes. The taste of the tea takes him back to childhood and his mother's house and a manless world of women visitors and card tables and small sandwiches and dressing-up. Butch remembers his own very plain face and handsome hair that was blonde and curly. And long as a girl's. Butch remembers his Granny drying his hair in a big pink towel and brushing it until it shone like spun gold. Spun gold! — that is what his Granny called it as she dried it and brushed it back from his forehead and pulled the sides down over his ears.

Butch drains his cup and remembers how his mother would always come and inspect Granny's handiwork. He remembers how his mother would tease his hair to make it curlier and curlier until he looked like a small albino version of a Zulu warrior. He remembers how his mother would always ask her lady friends if he wasn't just the prettiest boy they had ever seen. And he remembers how those ladies always agreed that he certainly was pretty even if they did not prize prettiness in a small boy to the degree that his mother and grandmother did. And he hears his mother interjecting with an odd mixture of pride and regret that sometimes she has to literally drive him out of the house to play since he'd rather stay inside even on sunny days and read the *Encyclopaedia Britannica*. And Butch sees himself bristling at those words. But bristling came later, much later, when he had actually started to read his way through the encyclopedia from beginning to end. In the days of the afternoon teas, in the days before he had been thrust out of the brick house on the Crescents into the larger world of school, he had

A Hole With A Head In It

loved being petted and admired by his mother and her friends.

Butch opens his eyes and looks at the bottom of his empty teacup and stares at the pattern of leaves and remembers that once he could and did read the future from tea leaves. In Granny's house no two cups are the same. Each cup is handpainted with different kinds of English garden flowers and every cup and saucer is shaped differently from its neighbour on the walnut tea wagon. But they are all rimmed with gold and he drinks his tea from a cup decorated with pansies. The rim is chipped. He drinks his tea at the kitchen table with Granny and as soon as they are done, they go back to the sittingroom and a place is cleared for them on the small settee and his mother's lady friends bring them their empty cups and Granny reads their fortunes in the tea leaves. Granny is clairvoyant and teaches him the secrets of her art: keep the handle to the left and use it as the starting point. Lines and symbols to the right side of the handle mean what the fates hold in store. Lines and symbols to the left are the things that come about through personal initiative. Acorns bring good luck. Anchors mean love. Angels are good news. Boots mean travel. Baskets are storks bringing babies. Brooms indicate changes, clean sweeps. Bulls are dangers. Florio is a Taurus but this comes later in the tea leaves, in life. Castles are legacies. Cats are ill-omened loves. Coffins indicate death. Circles are money. Under D, there are devils, and there are eggs under E and F has fountains, and Granny takes him in his pre-school days through her alphabet of signs until Butch has mastered her diviner's dictionary. And he saw anchors and angels and acorns in all their lives. Now he sees coffins, coffins, coffins everywhere.

Tonight in Montreal at Florio's, among the coffins, he sees in his cup an anchor, a love. He thinks suddenly not so much of new-found love as of an old seashore and sees boats riding in a harbour at high tide. They bobble and the bubble of memory bursts and he sighs and thinks back to other boats bobbling elsewhere. He is a lover of the sea and always takes a winter holiday to the sand and sun and anchors of the West Indies. St. Vincent. In the summers, he goes to San Francisco or to the Aegean. He has watched many boats bob at their anchors at high tide. He closes his eyes and recaptures the bubble of memory he most wants and sees inside it the Tancook Island ferry. It is a vivid memory of Nova Scotia five years ago. It wasn't a holiday. He was looking for Florio. In a way, he wishes he hadn't found him. In a way he wishes Florio was a past that he could revisit only in memory — dulled, distant memory. He straightens Florio's bedclothes and kisses his stubbly cheek, then stretches and presses his nose against the grimed glass of the studio window and studies the passing lights of the cars on The Main.

"I suppose your father could have your bed and you could take mine and I could sleep on the couch. How does that sound to you, Florio?"

"Don't fuss. Just leave things the way they are. He won't stay overnight. Trust me."

"But what if he wants to stay? It's no good you telling me to just leave things as they are because things aren't always the way you want them to be, are they? We don't know his plans, do we? He hasn't said, has he? If he comes here expecting a bed for the night, we'll have to put him somewhere, won't we? And I don't want him in my bedroom and I'm not going to have you sleeping with me while he's here in the house, and I just can't stand to see what it does to the couch or to you or to the front room when you spend the night in here. So we'll put him in your bed if he stays and you'll have mine and I'll sleep in here, right?"

"If that's the way you want it, that's the way we'll do it, if he stays the night."

"So now you think he may stay the night, do you?"

"No, I don't think that he's really going to want to spend the night under my roof. Stop fussing."

"But what if your father does want to stay? We can't just turn him away from the door, you know we can't."

"All the more reason to do it, isn't it? He expects me to be unconventional."

"It isn't a matter of unconventionality. It's hospitality. When parents come to visit, you give them a bed."

"Well, we're not going to do it. I really don't give a damn if it's the done thing or not. Just leave everything as it is. You don't have to give up your bed. I don't have to give up my bed. Nobody has to sleep on the couch. If he stays too late tonight to drive back to Halifax, he can stay at the Windjammer."

"At the height of the season? For God's sake, talk sense! I'm going to change the sheets on both beds just in case he does stay. I'm not going to have your father sleep in your dirt. You can be very annoying, you know."

"And you can make more of a fuss than the guy who's waiting for Godot, you know. Forget about my father. I made a reservation at the Windjammer just in case he needs a place. He wouldn't stay with us for love or money, Butchie Godot."

"Jesus, why didn't you say so in the first place! You can be a real pain in the ass."

"Don't you just wish, don't you just wish."

He was furious but Florio wasn't prepared to take any notice of him. Florio just burrowed deeper into the previous Sunday's *New York Times*, and he took his fury back upstairs to the room that faced that part of the Atlantic Ocean that is Mahone Bay. From the window he looked down on the yachts that filled its basin. Nearer, almost at his feet, he watched sturdy, squat, straight residents of Chester buy fresh fish on the docks, and taller, leaner, less upright tourists study the menus posted outside genteel restaurants that had established themselves as their nearest and least dear neighbours. Watching the tourists approach and the locals retreat, he felt sad enough to cry for the seedy part of town that was being reborn. He didn't want Chester to be a chic summer place. He looked out across the bay. The passenger ferry was starting out on its hourly voyage to Tancook Island. He felt so suddenly sad that he sat down at the piano and began to play.

    Grieg. He no longer played Grieg as well as he once did. Grieg required a certain softness and suppleness in the fingers that he'd lost. It wasn't the onset of middle age. It wasn't his anger against himself for his stupid quarrel with Florio. Mummy, like many other older people, managed to play Grieg well right into the arms of enraged senility. It wasn't getting older that had done it to him. It wasn't just plain tiredness. No matter how tired, how frustrated his mother had been at the end of a long day of teaching the rudiments of piano to small children with large-mouthed mothers, she had been able to make Grieg sing. She could still make Grieg sing. Butch cocked an ear to the piano and suspended his own playing and heard the way Mummy had taught him to play the piece. Lowering his fingers to the keyboard and playing, it sounded other than it should have sounded in the room and in his head. He punished his faulty fingers with great booming chords of his own invention. He hoped that he'd disturb Florio. He hoped that he'd force Florio to abandon his newspaper. He hoped that Florio would come upstairs and be kind to him, ravish him with kisses.

    Grieg. It was this music played on an old upright Steinway with a cracked soundboard and chipped yellow keys that first drew Florio to him in the school in which they were held captive. It pulled Florio away from his Scott's stamp catalogue and down the long dusty corridor from the junior recreation room and into the doorway of the more private room where he practised, where he was supposed to practise church music. But he made his own music. Outside chapel services, there was little music to be heard in the priest-run boarding school to which he had been confined after his Granny's death and his mother's move to her sister's house in Peterborough.

Grieg. Butch's Grieg. It was this music that brought Florio to him. It wasn't love. It wasn't friendship. Those came later. In the beginning, it was the boredom of Sunday afternoon broken by small melodious sounds that hinted at something larger.

Tires crunched against the gravel below the window. His fingers collapsed to silence as he listened for the sound of the car turning into the drive and stopping. Hearing it, he raced downstairs. Florio was unmoved and brooding within a messy nest of newspaper surmounted by a half-empty whisky decanter. There was solid hammering on the front door. "I'll get the door. You see to the newspapers. Please."

"Don't fuss so. My father isn't worth it. Me neither."

"Do shut up please and just pick up the damned funny papers."

"What funny papers? This is the *Times*."

"This isn't the time to argue. I'm getting the door."

They'd met only once before. Years and years ago. But Floyd Keller Senior flashed a tight smile of recognition, pumped his hand. "They still call you Butch, do they?"

"That's right, Mr. Keller. Do come in."

"I never forget a face. Hardly ever a name. Yours is George, isn't it?"

"I'm Butch to everybody since my Granny died," he said icily as he stared into Mr. Keller's face. He couldn't see anything of Florio's devastating handsomeness in it. Nor was there anything of the man he remembered meeting the one time that Mr. Keller had come to visit Florio at school. That man had seemed tall, ramrod straight, tough, leathery. An oil rigger. This man was just crumpled, paunchy, bald, florid in an expensive way. An Alberta oilman. Crude. Alberta crude. He felt Florio's hand on his shoulder, registered the flash of rage in Mr. Keller's eyes. He stepped aside quickly, played the role of peacemaker and host as effortlessly as he could in the circumstances. He got Mr. Keller a large glass of Coke over ice and poured himself a Perrier while Florio lowered the amber level of Scotch in the decanter by another inch.

Seated in the armchair, glass in hand, Mr. Keller talked to them as a man who wore a dark blue ultra-suede jacket with a lighter blue shirt and a tri-toned blue striped tie with grey ripcord trousers and tooled cowboy boots was inclined to talk, he supposed. Mr. Keller had an immense amount of small talk and he addressed it to a point on the wall behind his son's ears. He gave the spot on the wall an inning-by-inning account of a baseball game he'd seen in Montreal the previous evening. He told it about the cabbie who had taken him out to Olympic Stadium and the cabbie who brought him back to the Sheraton Centre. He told it of his dissatisfactions with Montreal's black taxi drivers. He told it of his great satisfaction with the Sheraton Centre. He told it of his distaste for parts of Montreal: St. Catherine Street was a drug and sex war zone. The Pope, he thought, was definitely to blame for the blatant sexuality of the place.

Perhaps the wall yawned but suddenly Mr. Keller was on to hockey. The wall must have been smiling encouragement. There was a torrent of tale-telling about the Edmonton Oilers. Inside stuff. The Oilers were his hometown team. They were winners. They were almost American. This led him to talk of the West Edmonton Mall, the largest dang shopping centre on the face of the earth. Florio yawned openly. Mr. Keller didn't seem to notice. He had the full and undivided attention of the friendly wall behind his son's head and began to lecture it on the virtues of the Free Market System, Supply Side Economics, Monetarism, Reaganism. Everything was Capitalized, everything was capital. Butch stared at the wall and felt blistered for its sake as Mr. Keller declaimed against creeping socialism, PetroCan, the Canadian dollar, Israel. But the wall

A Hole With A Head In It

had strengths he lacked and remained impassive. Despite his ingrained good manners, he began to slump in his chair and stare at his own fingers and think about how little music was left in them. He looked up and smiled and tried to focus on Mr. Keller's anti-Zionism but he'd missed a transition.

The children of Moses had given way to the sons and daughters of Jesus and the wall had ceased being the preferred audience. Mr. Keller was speaking directly to them. And it wasn't just Jerry Falwell and the Moral Majority and maybe-Jim-Keegstra-has-a-point-you-know. It was stranger and stronger than that: Mr. Keller had been baptized in the Blood of the Lamb. The Holy Spirit had newly descended upon him. He had been buried in the black waters and he had been reborn in the clear waters of the Resurrection. He had been born again. He was witnessing to Christ right there in the front room of the house in Chester by the waters of Mahone Bay. Butch was wide-awake in his worst nightmare — Florio's father was in their midst as an Avenging Angel. He felt hot and clammy, wet with fear.

With a pocket-sized New Testament open in his hand, Mr. Keller was saying, "Listen boys, this is not my word. This is not the word of any man. This is God's own word. And it says, 'The wages of sin is death.' Right here, it says that, just that, 'The wages of sin is death.' But no man has to die. All men are born to everlasting life. It says so, right here. And all you have to do to have eternal life is simply to accept the Lord Jesus Christ into your life. And if you want to accept the Lord Jesus Christ into your life, all you have to do is to kneel right down beside me and say, 'Lord Jesus, come into my heart,' and when He hears your prayer, He'll enter right into you and make you well. I've seen Him do it. I've seen Him enter men and women and drive the uncleanness right out of them. I've seen the downcast uplifted and the bent straightened."

Mr. Keller paused, looked deeply into his New Testament and sifted its words for words that would not fall on stony ground. "I tell you that I've seen men as queer as any you have ever met accept Christ into their hearts. Those men are married now and are the fathers of fine children. Floyd, will you kneel down beside me now, son, and pray with me? And you too, George?"

Floyd. George. The old names, the names of christening pierced like bullets into Butch's brain. Floyd Joseph Paul Keller. George Anthony Benet. But they weren't bullets, there was no sense of violence in Mr. Keller, just the pathetic hopefulness of the true believer. The nightmare had come to very little. Still, Florio rose from the sofa like a great breaker from the sea and swept across the room to Mr. Keller and clenched him by the shoulders and spat in his face. Full in his face. Then the wave that was Florio retreated as suddenly as it had swept forward and it broke out the door and ran out to the wharf.

Face to the window, red with embarrassment, Butch followed Florio's passage and watched him jump aboard the Tancook Island ferry. At his back, he heard Mr. Keller say, "I only want to help him. I only wish him the happiness of his own children. If he had daughters of his own, his mother would live again in them and he'd be free of her ghost. He needs a wife and daughters. He doesn't really need you, George. Let him go, please."

He looked at Florio's father. Mr. Keller's face was white and crestfallen with a purple-red tracery of broken veins in his cheeks. He wasn't made of granite. He was travertine — soft and porous. Butch opened the window. He hoped fresh sea air would turn Mr. Keller to dust. It didn't. When he turned around and faced the room, Mr. Keller was sobbing into a large white handkerchief. He wasn't altogether certain what he could or should say. Florio's gesture had been so crude and melodramatic as to hint of something more deeply felt. Not knowing what to say, he said the things he'd been taught by his Granny to say in awkward circumstances of any sort. It did the trick. Florio's father waxed nostalgic, showed him photographs of Junior as an infant, told him stories of infancy when

A Hole With A Head In It

Floyd Junior was so small and frail he, heh-heh, had to be basted with olive oil and kept in a roasting pan in the warming oven to keep him warm enough to live through his first prairie winter.

After Mr. Keller had left, Butch returned to the upper room and its piano but he did not play. He gripped his knees with his hands and stared at the hard black and white keys. Ebony and ivory. "Ebony and Ivory." Paul McCartney. Stevie Wonder. The harmony of perfect opposites. Florio's music, not his. Florio's blindness, not his own, had gripped him until Florio had returned a little repentant and much too late.

3

The Main is quieter now. He turns away from the window. Wrapped in bedclothes dampened with sweat, Florio sleeps fitfully. He mumbles, he jerks, he calls out a name — Evelyn. He repeats it at intervals in moans and cries and whispers. It is the name of a dead woman whom Butch never met. He cannot summon memories of her to his friend's bedside. Not in the flesh. He has never known her as she existed outside Florio's imagination. He knows her only as Florio has painted her in the neo-expressionist paintings that now litter this studio. In them, Evelyn exists as a fierce shadow that has blacked out Florio's customary painterly concerns. In them, she exists as a blood-red muse that has exploded Florio's painterly reputation for lightness and clarity of expression. She is the face of death that Yuppie gallery owners outbid one another to see gracing their large white walls. Evelyn is the woman that Mr. Keller's prayers seemed to will upon Florio. He straightens the bedclothes and wipes the sweat from Florio's face. He would like him to wake but he doesn't.

While Florio sleeps, Butch seeks out Evelyn in the canvas images but he cannot find the once-living being behind the paint. He would like to see at least one true-to-life photograph of her. He tells himself that if he could see her, he could better help Florio cope with the memory of her. He suspects that some concrete sign of the nebulous figure in the paintings is to be found in the locked box that Florio has brought back from the house on Mahone Bay. Not finding images and souvenirs of Evelyn elsewhere in his trips around the studio, he has convinced himself that they are to be found in the locked box half-hidden under Florio's bed. It is a large box and very heavy and he has to get down on his hands and knees and exert considerable force to slide it out from under the bed and into the middle of the room. He has done this several times in the last few days, but each time he has done so he has returned the box unopened to its storage space. The box is roughly carpentered, and a protruding nailhead keeps digging into the floorboards and scrapes long ragged scars that he repeatedly scrubs out with a paint-soaked rag from a bucket beside the smallest of Florio's easels. It has been the automatic reaction of a person who has been doing things he would be ashamed to be caught doing. But really, there is no one to catch him at it, is there? Florio will probably not wake till morning now, right?

He inspects the box once more. It is a fairly ordinary wooden box of the kind that his generation of university students used to pack and ship books from home to school and back again. It is constructed out of a single sheet of half-inch plywood, a length of one-by-one pine, two hinges, a hasp, a handful of screws, and two short lengths of rope for handles. It will never be an object of beauty but it has been made interesting by the shipping labels it has accumulated as Florio has trundled it from one art college to another, from one studio to the next, from life with one lover to life with another. Beneath the labels, there is a worn coating of black paint.

Florio is open if not entirely truthful about almost everything in his life and always has been with Butch. But he has not been open about this box and the things it contains. In all the years he has known Florio to have owned the box, it has never once been opened in his presence and it has always been kept locked with a stout padlock. He now has the key in his hand. All he needs to do is to insert the key and turn it and remove padlock from hasp and lift the lid, and all of Florio's secrets will be his for the taking. He wishes it weren't this easy. He wishes the box were covered with dustballs. He imagines sweeping the lid with the back of his hand and watching the grey turn black and spiderwebby. He thinks of himself rummaging for a clean rag and wiping both the back of his hand and then the exposed surfaces of the box. But all he has to do is to insert the key and turn it. He inserts the key, he turns it, the padlock falls open. He slides it from the staple. He lays it aside. He lifts the lid and the light falls on a welter of notebooks and large brown envelopes and loose photographs. Layered like the remains of an ancient empire, the most recent lie closest to hand. He turns layer upon layer upside down on the floor beside the box until nothing stands between himself and the time he went in search of Florio and found him living in the house on Mahone Bay and Mr. Keller came to visit.

The first photograph is of Florio on the Tancook Island ferry, his back to the mainland. He is smiling with a familiar lust. The object of his lust is obviously the person holding the camera and that persona is obviously Evelyn, for it is she who is the subject of the thick layer of photographs accompanying it. In some, she is dressed; in others, she is semi-dressed; in the rest, she is undressed.

Naked, Evelyn is a narrow young woman, elongated in head and body. Her neck is thin, blunt, chiselled into high squared shoulders that frame the flat planes of her chest. Her breasts are small knobs that tilt upward no matter which way the rest of her leans. Two-thirds of the knobs are dark nipple. Like a boy, Evelyn is straight to the hips and flares out angularly. Her pelvic bones rise against her flesh like ploughshares. Are they the swords that pierced Florio's heart? Is there ever any understanding of heterosexual passion? It is only in her lower groin and her legs that Evelyn becomes curvaceous. Her legs are long and beautiful. Looking at them, admiring them, he thinks of the women who model stockings for Hanes. He thinks also of his mother. Mummy's legs are still very fine. He does not have his mother's legs but he does have his mother's perfectly formed feet. He smiles broadly as he notices that Evelyn's beautiful legs terminate in large ruined feet. He cannot imagine Florio kissing those arches, sucking those toes like Florio has kissed his arches and sucked his toes. Florio is capable of many things but sexually, he is always aesthetic. If her feet are not an attraction, what in her is?

Butch is drawn to the clump of black hair at her groin and the lighter clumps of hair in her armpits and the great shaggy mop of bleached hair that envelops her head. Hair has always been the thing that has been most seductive. He thinks of Florio's rich mat of chest hair. He thinks of the ways in which it can be twisted around his finger. He goes back to thinking of Evelyn. It is her hair that would attract him if he were attracted to her. But he is not attracted to her in her nakedness.

Semi-naked, Evelyn is curvaceous calves sloping into curving thighs creasing lace and satin lingerie into narrow tight folds. This is somewhat more attractive but what is a body without a face? Nothing! Faces are everything to him, more than hair. It is faces that he loves and it is only in the pictures of Evelyn fully dressed that he sees her face. To him, a human face is as full of signs and portents of fate and destiny as the bottom of a teacup. But Evelyn's face is an empty cup against which he recoils. How, he wonders, could Florio have loved such a face? Perhaps it was personality, perhaps it was the things she had to say, could say, did say that drew Florio to her. Florio can always be drawn sexually with words, with music. Perhaps she sang? He digs deeper, shifts from pictures to a poem carefully printed in an unfamiliar hand in a lined schoolbook:

> A sand mite bites the heel you fed with kisses
> i hurry over the rise and fall before the bed

A Hole With A Head In It

> of heaven, its sheets still troubled by storms
> of your making in my mouth:
> Uncouth i turn to the beach with feet
> ploughing furrows in the young dunes:
> The altar of the beach has no candles,
>   no books, no incense
> just a priesthood of fine young men tumbling
>   in front
> a candy-striped tabernacle. Rosy. Crossed, they
>   bruise
> their thighs, toss balls high in the air.
> My jaw throbs where you entered me
> i watch balls sail above the ocean
> with their dog wetted liver brown and fiercely
>   proud
> my jaw throbs where you entered me
> picture Picasso here with me drawing me out

and then a single scrawled line of ink outlining an animal form that might be a dog with a crown on its head and a belly full of puppies or perhaps a goat half-liquid with milk.

   Butch does not know, cannot say because the drawing is, in his estimation, pretty piss poor. And the poem? He goes back and reads it again and tries to see a meaning beyond that which seems to him obvious: after a night of lovemaking in which oral sex has played a prominent part, Evelyn rests her sore jaws by watching young men play volleyball on the beach; she adopts their dog for company and it all puts her in mind of something she has seen somewhere by Picasso. Or is the artistic reference something just dropped in to make it more appealing to Florio? Who knows? Who cares? What is there really to care about in any contemporary poetry, he asks himself. The real poets nowadays are the songwriters. Has any living poet written lines as good as Tom Waits's? Thinking about it, Butch starts running the lyrics of "The One That Got Away" through his memory and wishes that he could so simply say of Evelyn that she was a dead issue, an open coffin in a closed case. But he can't, and so he returns to her poem, sifts the pages of the notebook some more, encounters this:

> i cross my eyes find the point of power
> in it i place myself straight eyes closed
> i count the breaths of a dinosaur daddy
> dada like birds of a feather
> whores flock together
> sing a song of puppy love
> the dog has left its manger
> if you sing along with me
> i won't feel any stranger

He reads no further. He has read enough, he thinks, to get a handle on the kind of poet and person she is, was, for Florio. She was a whore, Florio! She was a whore with a heart as twisted by psychological complexities as any woman, as all women her age are, Florio! He dismisses her and wishes the night were over, Florio awake and feeling better, getting better, recovering, and this detritus of another life could be forgotten, hidden away, rammed and jammed back in its box, consigned to a rubbish tip, incinerated, destroyed, whatever. But that cannot be and so he plunges deeper into the box, uncovers layers of life long before Evelyn entered the picture. He digs deep, deep down in the box, turns up a picture of Rue Ontario.

Rue Ontario. It could have been the title of a manifesto if the English artists and musicians of the French Quarter had been given to making public pronouncements, but it was only the name of a nondescript street transecting the district. There were jazz clubs in semi-basements and workingclass diners and hole-in-the-wall needletrade workshops and sprawling capacious coldwater flats over automobile parts suppliers that smelled of rubber and grease. Butch had his own flat on Rue Ontario and gave parties that were open to whoever found the way to his

A Hole With A Head In It

door. He gave many parties, was spendthrift with the money Granny had given him so that he could study music at McGill and qualify as a music teacher in case his performance skills were not up to the standard his mother had willed into him. And it was there, in the middle of a party, that Florio walked back into his life after four years of heart-breaking absence and abstinence. Florio had been studying in Italy with sculptors of old-fashioned outlook and temper and training. With them, he had studied anatomy — practical and theoretical. With them, he had mastered the science of calibrating the body top to toe. With them, he had learned to celebrate the male body, front and back. He had learned the effects of aging and dissipation on flesh and muscle. He had broken his right arm in four places when his Vespa was run into the face of a cliff by a drunken industrialist in a Mercedes. An industrialist who, Florio later claimed, had taken him to a villa high in the hills while he recuperated.

This industrialist, he alleged, had been married to a very famous Roman model. They had formed a ménage à trois. It had been very exciting. Both man and wife had catered to his every whim, in and out of bed. He gained whole new continents of sensation from this experience but he did not regain his full strength in his right hand. He had given up sculpture; he had turned to painting. He had returned to Canada. He had returned to his first and greatest love.

Back from Italy, in Butch's world of Rue Ontario, Florio stood out. While the other artists grew their hair shoulder-length and stopped shaving, Florio went to a Sicilian barber every week and had his hair cut close against the scalp with a straight razor and the ends singed with flaming sulphurous matchsticks. On his upper lip, the barber crafted a perfect rectangle of clipped whiskers. While others wore sandals and jeans and workshirts and oversized sweaters and carried knapsacks, Florio wore grey suits and black shirts and bright ties and European loafers and carried an ancient leather briefcase. While others talked about Chicago blues bands, Florio combed second-hand record stores for albums featuring the jazz pianist Bill Evans. While other painters on Rue Ontario slavishly imitated the most abstract of their teachers' expressions without altogether forsaking the impressionism of the old guard, Florio quarrelled with everyone at art school. He was thought a philistine because he admitted to watching more than hockey games on television. But he could not be ignored; he had a huge talent for realism, he had a wonderful capacity for self-promotion, he had a scathing tongue and articulate principles, and he was the first in that set to openly embrace bisexuality. He knew exactly who he was and what he was capable of doing. Butch admired him. Butch was unable to articulate much of anything about himself or his music and he could not say anything of the love that consumed him and the appetites that ruined him for women. He responded the best way he knew how: he became a Bill Evans imitator.

He sighs at the memory of it, at the memory of a time in Montreal when nobody could make a living playing jazz. It is into those days and those appetites that he most wants to retreat in his thoughts as he drifts into sleep slumping over Florio's box. Drifting sleepwards, Butch is grasped and held under the control of a foreign power. Evelyn's power? A pair of eyes float eerily over the sheaves of photographs and leaves of paper. The eyes are depressingly blank, drugged. He tries to find lips, ears, nose, nostrils, cheeks, chin to attach to the eyes but there is only a jaw, an uncompromising jut of jaw. A voice tells him that Evelyn's cheeks are the cutting edges of a determined mind, that her nose is a wedge that sunders all opposition, that her nostrils are a sea of nervous energy, that her ears are tight coils of stubbornness. A voice tells him that Evelyn is his opposite. He does not believe this voice. Florio's emotional range is narrow, he tells himself, and Florio has loved them both. But then he is crying and his tears nudge him back into consciousness and the words from a song on the T Bone Burnett album replaying itself in the background comes clearly into his mind and shakes him awake.

4

Butch returns to the teapot and pours himself another cup and thinks about clearing up the mess he has made of Florio's things and about putting himself properly to bed for the night. The long-case clock has struck one. He returns to the box by the bedside and begins to replace all that it contains. In his haste to do so, he plunges his right hand deep down and, through a miscalculation of distance to the floor, jams his fingers. A searing pain takes his breath away.

It is Sunday afternoon, the boys have been given a free afternoon, and everyone wants to head downtown and see a movie. But some people don't want other people to tag along with them, so Florio gets dumped upside down into a garbage can full of cold baked beans and potato parings behind the refectory. And Butch comes to his aid immediately and tries to dislodge him, but Florio thinks it is one of his attackers returning and flails and kicks and topples the can with a horrendous crash and clatter and a stream of profanity.

Father Prefect overhears and comes quickly out from the priest's parlour but does not comprehend the situation and frog-marches both boys to his office and lectures them on the need in boys their age for good physical exercise that toughens the body and fortifies the soul. They are deprived of their liberty and exiled to the baseball diamond where Father Prefect, garbed in a white T-shirt and black trousers and white tennis shoes, waits with a baseball bat and more boys. It is not their first experience of this kind of detention. Butch is outfitted with shinguards and a catcher's mitt and a facemask and a chest protector. The other boys are given outfielders' gloves. Florio is handed the ball. Father Prefect takes the one and only bat in hand and swaggers up to the plate. The boys arrange themselves around the diamond. They will stay there until they make three outs against Father Prefect's batting. They will stay there all afternoon. Father Prefect once had a tryout with the Brooklyn Dodgers as a left-handed first baseman and played a couple of seasons of double A. Father Prefect makes them run three laps around the outfield after each of the outs. Butch plays catcher because there is almost nothing for him to do behind the plate. Father Prefect swings at everything that isn't beyond the reach of the catcher. Florio pitches. Father Prefect hits and hits and hits and then there is a liner that screams through the infield knocking Florio from the mound before being snagged in the webbing of the shortstop's glove. An out.

"Three laps around the outfield boys. No walking. No talking."

They huff and they puff and drag themselves into home plate and then drag themselves back into position and someone else pitches, and Butch has nothing to catch as Father hits and hits and hits as he finds his groove and stays in it. And then, the unexpected: a foul tipped to the catcher's glove is caught and held despite the flame of pain that brings tears to Butch's eyes. He hurls the mitt and ball into the dust and plunges his fingers to his mouth.

"Put that mitt back on, fellow, and get back into position. You could have had an easy out. Remember, a man who can play with a little pain is always a winner in life. Play ball."

And the pitcher pitches before the batter and Butch are ready and it comes straight into the catcher's mitt and snaps his wrist backwards. The world goes black and a jagged white line divides it down the middle.

Florio visits him in the infirmary and gives him a teddy bear as a present. Butch has three broken bones in his left hand. He can still feed himself but Florio wants to do something to make him feel better than even a teddy bear can make him feel, so he lets Florio spoon food into his mouth like a mother does for her child. But Florio cries and Butch strokes his arm and then the food is put aside and they are holding one another tight and kissing like children do as they crush the teddy bear between them. A shadow falls over them and Father Prefect stands between them and the light and snarls, "That's not the way for men to behave, lads. We'll have none of that, we'll have none of that ever again. You'll both be men before I'm done with you." And the teddy bear is confined to a cupboard inside Father Prefect's office until Graduation Day.

All of this returns in an instant and with it the full force of the hatred he feels against so many elements of the past he shares with Florio. Had it not been for that school, they would never have met in the ordinary course of things. That is the only good Butch has ever been able to attribute to their schooling. The priests were reputed to be civilized men and they undoubtedly knew many fine things from the foreign worlds in which they had travelled. But those travels and studies had also diminished the practical sense within them. When it came to handling boys, when it came to fulfilling their holy function to act *in loco parentis*, the priests became cruder than the crudest of parents. It has taken years and years for him to begin to make even a little sense of what that school did to him and to Florio and to untold others.

The priests gave everybody a new name for a start and the nicknames they bestowed were seldom honorific, frequently satirical and always descriptive in a sneering sort of way — even the brightest "Brains" among them was brought low by his moniker. And along with the names went attitudes as rough as any found on the prairies when it was still frontier: the priests, despite their education, sponsored cruel practical jokes, allowed ugly prejudices, systematically persecuted individualism in any form, and bullied all sensitivities. Why? Why had they had been levellers rather than uplifters of the human spirit? It was not enough simply to say that religion had taught them that young boys were allies of the devil. There was more to it. There was something far more primitive in their responses to the boys, something that had to do with contempt for all living things, something that allowed them to eat great semi-raw hunks of beefsteak at every opportunity, something that allowed them to feed the boys in their charge any vile thing that was not actively poisonous. He reins in his thoughts and runs cold water over his fingers to take away the sting of past and present misadventure. The priests were as cruel and as crude as cowboys and far less romantic.

Cowboyism. It is this as much as anything that makes him loathe the effect Evelyn has had on Florio. She has done to him what the priests had never been able to do to him: she has split Florio away from his friendship and love, she has returned Florio to far too much of the world that they had bravely withstood in priests and fellow students. Under Evelyn's influence, Florio has exchanged suits and ties for denims and cowboy boots. Butch can see the boots — four pairs of them — neatly aligned alongside Florio's full-length mirror. Under her influence, Florio has exchanged all the music that Butch had given him for Ricky Scaggs and Randy Travis, K.T. Oslin and k.d. lang, Nanci Griffiths, the Sweethearts of the Rodeo, Dwight Yoakum and David Lynne Jones, Ian Tyson, Ricky Van Shelton, the O'Kanes, Steve Earle and dozens more. Under her influence, Florio has grown nostalgic and paternalistic and paternal and sentimental about dogs and children. Under her influence, for all he knows, Florio might even have gone horseback riding. And it is this recognition that he does not know enough about her yet that sends him back to the box and the layers of Florio's life that can be seen and studied.

Early in January 1984, Florio started a half-year sabbatical from his college teaching job in Montreal by moving to

A Hole With A Head In It

Nova Scotia and renting a house in Chester. The house was the property of an art historian from Boston and contained everything Florio hoped such a house would contain: there was wine in the cellar, Danish cutlery and earthen tableware in the kitchen, garden produce and wild berries in a freezer on the enclosed back porch, cupboards stocked with home preserves, well-worn furniture covered with bright throws and cushions from New Mexico, an out-of-tune Steinway in an upstairs room filled with sheet music, and an almost antique but still faithful stereo together with a huge collection of Deutsche Grammaphon Archiv recordings plus the best of the British Invasion — Beatles, Stones, The Who. There was also a fully equipped artist's studio in a third floor attic naturally lit by oversize skylights. The only thing wrong with the house was that the heating system was inadequate everywhere except in the attic. So Florio pulled an old couch into the studio and flung a sleeping bag on top of it and forgot about the rest of the house except the kitchen. He was happy to be on his own. He made lists of things he wanted to accomplish. He made drawings for the paintings he intended to paint. He discovered a plethora of photographic equipment and a bathroom that did double duty as a darkroom.

February was a time of severe winter storms and Florio was unused to the Maritime winter. The storms terrified him. He cowered inside the house and hoped against hope that the power wouldn't fail but it did. Repeatedly. At the end of February, with the arrival of the worst storm and the longest blackout, he gave up and jammed a few things into a rucksack and drove to Halifax airport in an old truck that came with the house. But just before his flight to Montreal was called, it was cancelled. Another storm was sweeping into the region. Florio was despondent. Lacking the will to do anything else, he sat down in the lounge. The place was jammed with Newfoundlanders, stranded but carefree. The authorities were urging everyone to take a bus back to town and wait out the storm at a Halifax hotel. Florio returned to his truck and found a young woman sitting inside. She told him she hated crowds as if this explained everything. If he was going back to Halifax, she told him, he could give her a lift. He gave her a lift all the way to Chester and his house and she entered his life as they shook the wet and tiredness from themselves, opened a jug of the art historian's best home-made wine, heaped a whole lot of bedding on a big double bed and crawled inside and got gloriously drunk.

The woman told Florio that her name was Early Spring. This was a joke. Her name was Evelyn Airleigh Sprung. This was not a joke: she had a Vermont driver's licence to prove she was who she said she was, although she also had a fistful of credit cards in other names. As a joke of his own, Florio called her Cinnamon because she sprinkled that spice on everything she ate — including his private parts.

Evelyn Airleigh Sprung travelled light. She brought with her the clothes that she wore, a carry-all, a handbag. When she first undressed and shivered her way into Florio's bed, she was wearing a pair of lime-green lowcut Sporto Portage Pacs. Portage Pacs are reputed to keep feet warm and dry because they have uppers of oil-treated chrome-tanned leather that is supposed to defy mud, rain and snow. These uppers are triple-stitched to bottoms of vulcanized gum rubber with crepe rubber soles for traction, gum rubber dyed the same shade of Soviet green as Lada paints on some of their cars. It was these shoes that interested Florio the most of all her possessions. They were the only thing practical about her. Her socks were out at heel, her dress was summer-weight cotton, her home-knit woollen sweater of many stripes and more dropped stitches was threadbare, her coat was a moth-nibbled fur jacket with a rip under the right armhole and missing buttons. She had no scarf nor hat nor gloves. But in her carry-all, she carried a black silk dance dress slit high on the thigh, black lace underwear, a pair of thong sandals with high high heels, an Oriental shawl, squares of Chinese silk, costume jewelry, belts, an ebony cigarette holder, a copy of Rimbaud's *Une saison en enfer:*

A Hole With A Head In It

> J'ai de mes ancêtres gaulois l'oeil bleu blanc, la
> cervelle étroite, et la maladresse dans la lutte.
> Je trouve mon habillement aussi barbare que le leur.
> Mais je ne beurre pas mas chevelure . . .

which she had translated in the margin

> White-blue-eyed I of my Gallic
> past narrow-skulled clumsiness
> my clothes are as barbaric
> but I don't butter my hair . . .

Later, she gave him poetry of her own, but then, just then, she produced a brass pipe and hashish and a drug-induced end to February: Evelyn Airleigh Sprung's handbag contained uppers, downers, LSD, Angel Dust, Demerol, cocaine. There were also edible lotions and perfumes. She slept with a switchblade knife under her pillow alongside her packet of contraceptive pills.

March. Evelyn sat and knitted for hours on end. Then she unravelled all that she had knitted. When she did this, she insisted that Florio call her Penelope Homebody. He thought this was very funny. Sometimes she pored over technical photography books all through the night and then confessed she had never owned a camera. Sometimes she pretended not to eat anything for whole days on end even though Florio found the empty preserve jars exactly where she had half-hidden them. Florio was infatuated by her freakiness, her bullying sexuality and her drugs. He loved her indifference to time and space, her photogenic postures in bed, her games with his mind.

5

Butch sits at Florio's bedside and reads all this in a diary Florio has kept of those days and nights of Nova Scotia winter. As he reads, he keeps filleting photos of Evelyn from the pile he discarded earlier. He continues to discard the ones of her undressed. He is interested in her face, in her eyes. But Evelyn's eyes are depressingly blank, drugged. He looks at her lips, ears, nose, nostrils, cheeks, chin. Again and again he notices that her jaw is an uncompromising jut, her cheeks are cutting edges of a determined mind, her nose is a wedge that sunders opposition, her nostrils are full of nervous energy, her ears are coils of stubbornness. Butch knows that he will never understand her and marvels that Florio can seemingly love her. The diary says he tells her he loves her, over and over. The diary says they talk of getting a dog. The diary says they talk of having a child.

To comfort himself, Butch mashes bananas in a bowl and makes a stack of peanut butter and banana sandwiches and eats them while he reads more of Evelyn's poetry.

> The house within the house
> is rich with the silks and velvets
> of the rising sun lace curtains and patchwork
> a negress sleeps on a four poster bed
> a poet fluffs her pillow
> all rhymes turn reasonable in violent light
> stroke me to sleep I am washed with snow
> I am a loaf of bread I am salt in the water
> I am burned with moonshine
> what kind of deal will you give the dealer?

April. May. Both months are missing. June. In June, Butch came to Nova Scotia in search of Florio. For several weeks, Florio hadn't answered letters. There was no telephone, no point of contact. Worried, as soon as one gig ended and before another started, Butch was on a flight to Halifax and in a rental car to Chester. He found Florio living on his own and making a mess of it. The house was squalid. Florio was in a very odd mood, lifeless, stale, enervated. He couldn't paint. He seemed haunted by a ghost that he would not name. And then Mr. Keller's telegram arrived, and then he came. And Florio spat in his face and fled the house and jumped aboard the Tancook Island ferry. And Butch consoled Mr. Keller as best he could and Mr. Keller went away and Florio returned from Tancook Island, a little repentant and very late and they fought.

What a battle!

Butch told Florio that there was no excuse for what he had done to his father. And Florio said there was.

In the fifties, Keller had been a geologist employed by the Standard Oil Company to manage an exploration rig in Alberta, far north of the Drumheller fields. It was very isolated — there were no towns, no schools, no other children. But Florio — Floydie as he was then — was happy. He watched the riggers drill test holes. They were muscular sunburnt men in sweat-stained undershirts and filthy chinos and heavy steel-toed boots. They teased him mercilessly but did anything and everything he asked them to do. They had children of their own, most of them, but those children were far away in Montana and Ohio and Texas. Floydie was their mascot.

They sometimes dragged him along when they played ball against the crews on neighbouring rigs. But mostly they kept him awake at night as they sat by their campfires and swapped tales about booze-ups and wide-legged women daft as geese. Floydie's mother hated him listening to such things from such low company. She wanted him to sit quietly beside her and fall asleep listening to the things she had to tell him about a very different kind of people — her kind of people — the ladies and gentlemen of England's Home Counties. She told him that gentlemen never lied and never bragged and never ever discussed women in a low way and always played cricket with a real bat, not with the sort of club these boorish men used in rounders. She would not call it baseball.

In the morning, Mrs. Keller taught him bits of mathematics, history, Latin, geography and literature. Literature was her greatest love and ally. And sketching. She taught him to sketch the wilderness in a pretty way. Twice she took Floydie back to England with her and stayed with her father. His grandfather Kendall rode to hounds, glorious in a red coat and high black boots.

Oil had been found. Maybe. There was sour gas. For certain. It was August and it was afternoon and it was hot and filthy and stinking at the well-head. Floydie brought the news from his father to his mother, who was reclining within the cool shade and artificial air of the trailer — his mother insisted upon calling it a caravan — that housed them. His mother just shrugged and gave him a tall glass of lemonade with a cube of ice, and mixed herself the same but added lots and lots of gin. He sat down beside her and let her hand ruffle his long blonde hair and pet him. Mr. Keller burst through the door, filthy with grime and roaring with excitement. It was an uncommon sight. Mr. Keller was in the habit of washing up outside at the stream with his men and changed both his clothes and manners before solemnly entering the trailer. Caravan.

Now, Keller stood there, stiff and angular, in clothes that stank of oil. Crude. Face-smudged, he had something to say but couldn't say it. He was too happy. "We've hit it. We've hit it. We've hit it," he repeated. When he could speak, he said, "Honey, I've been on the field phone. They want to see us in Texas. Then you and me are going to have a holiday, Peg."

Floydie wanted to jump up and dance around the room with his father but his mother's arms gripped him like thin steel cables. She said, "But what about the boy? Have you thought about Floydie in all this?"

"Of course, I have, Peg! What kind of man do you think I am? I arranged everything last week. I could feel the oil. I knew we were going to hit it big. Floydie will be going away to boarding school. We've put it off long enough. I've talked to the priests. He's half a year underage but they'll take him as a favour to me."

"You've arranged it, have you? Without asking? You want to take everything from me. You want to kill the child

A Hole With A Head In It

in him. You want to crush me. I might as well kill myself as have you do it. I tell you, you shan't do it, I won't have it, I'll kill myself first." Her mouth frothed with anger. Floydie could not break free of her grip. He looked at her lips and thought of her spittle as meringue. Lemon meringue was his favourite kind of pie.

"If the strike is as big as I think it is, we'll be able to send him to England to study with the Greyfriars in a year or two but the money isn't there right now, Peg, as you bloody well know. Besides, we need some time together, you and me, girl. And he needs friends his own age. Other boys. You can see that, can't you?"

But she couldn't.

Suddenly aware of his son, Keller caught hold of Floydie's arm and wrested him free. "Go play outside!"

Floydie hurried off to the bushes by the stream, to his special hiding place. He stayed hidden for a long time.

"Floydie, son, your mother — women — are the devil." His father, sweating, red-faced, out of breath, found him. "I love your mother, Floydie, you do know that, don't you? But it can stare her right in the face and she can't see it. This isn't England. You're almost a teenager — you need to be with boys your own age. What is the sense in talking about England? I won't have her father educating my son to be a smarmy Englishman. And do you think she'd stay here with me where she belongs beside her husband if you were in England? A wife is supposed to stand beside her husband. When we married, she swore before God that we would raise you as a Catholic and a Catholic you are going to be. Tomorrow, we'll drive into town. The three of us. The priests gave me a list of things you'll need to have at school. It's a good school. Go show your mother just how happy you are. I know you don't want to leave us. But no one ever wants to leave home that first time. Your mother will come around. She's in a funk now but we've seen her in a funk before, haven't we?"

There was screaming coming from the caravan. Floydie ran and stumbled and crashed to his knees at the threshold and fell inside. From the floor, Floydie could see straight through into the bathroom. He saw his mother. She, too, was on the floor. Her mouth was open and screaming. At the sight of him, she put her hands to her face. They dripped blood.

That was the end of his childhood.

That was the seminal experience in his life.

His mother meant to save him. She botched the job. She didn't even kill herself. She simply went mad.

Butch had not believed the story and said so.

Florio announced grandly that he was growing fonder of women than men. Some women friends meant a great deal more to him than most of his men friends. He announced that he was on his way to becoming a father. He announced that he was thinking seriously about getting married.

Butch had packed his bags and had walked out of Florio's life forever and ever amen.

Hah! What a joke that was. The two of them might separate but they could never divorce. Too much held them together, had always held them together, would hold them together until death. Florio had never before spoken so emotionally of fatherhood and family life. Butch attributed all of that to whatever it was that had gone on between Florio and his father. And it had seemed a reasonable assumption at the time. He had not known Evelyn beyond the mere fact that there was a woman somewhere bearing Florio's offspring within her. It had not moved him very much to know of his, had not moved him in the way he should have been moved. He had felt betrayed. He had felt jealous. He had felt enraged. He had not felt sympathetic. He had not felt compassionate. He had not felt joy that Florio was bringing something new and vital into the world, someone who would outlive them and keep their memory alive in ways that music and paintings never could. He had felt abandoned and left alone. And he had left Florio alone.

And so it had been from mutual friends and not from Florio himself that he had heard of the deaths of the woman and her child. The baby was stillborn. Evelyn had died a week afterwards of complications. And love had failed once more and he had not come running back to Nova Scotia. Those deaths had not healed the breach between them. It had broadened it. Away from the friendly and familiar influence Butch had always brought to bear on him, Florio went strange, very strange, turned his art into a shrine to the memory of Evelyn, turned the shrine into a money-grubbing business and turned his life as an artist into a career as empty and as junky as the Yuppie culture that now controlled The Main. And in all these turnings, Florio had kept his back to Butch, never once called out for help and consolation.

6

Butch is disturbed by the way his mind is running, by the fact that he cannot keep his thoughts straighter, more focused. He knows that he has to come to better terms with Evelyn and her dead daughter. He knows that he cannot delay any longer. He knows that he must work his way free of the woman of the poems, of the notebooks, of the photographs, of the paintings.

Evelyn seems a madwoman to him. What were her poems but hysteria? What was her sex except obsessions? But none of this really matters. What matters is to be as dispassionate about her as possible. Without this, how can he help Florio?

Butch needs a refuge. Buddhists, Florio once taught him, have three refuges. Buddhists take refuge in the Buddha, in the company of monks and in the Four Noble Truths: life is suffering; suffering has a cause; the cause of suffering is desire; desire can be overcome by following the Eightfold Path. One must seek right action and right speech and right understanding will follow and flow into right alertness, right . . .

There are steps to the path that he cannot remember but Butch does remember that life according to the Buddha is a river never returning. A rio flows. Florio. Florio is his refuge, his monastery, his law of life. This has always been the case, this will always be the case until death parts them finally and irrevocably.

> The function of the artist is to disturb. His duty is to arouse the sleepers, to shake the complacent pillars of the world. He reminds the world of its dark ancestry, shows the world its present, and points the way to a new birth. He is at once the product and the preceptor of his time. After his passage we are troubled and made unsure of the too easily accepted realities. He makes uneasy the static, the set and the still. In a world terrified of change, he preaches revolution — the principle of life. He is an agitator, a disturber of the peace — quick, impatient, positive, restless and disquieting. He is the creative spirit working in the soul of man.

Dr. Norman Bethune's words emerge from Florio's box. They are in Butch's own handwriting on the pale blue paper of an aerogram — a five-year-old aerogram postmarked from the villa in the south of France where he fled with a hard rugged pick-up love after the debacle in Nova Scotia. There are pin holes in the top and bottom of the aerogram. Is it something Florio pinned to the wall of his studio at Mahone Bay?

Bethune's words once meant something very important to him — why else had he so scrupulously copied them out by hand on an aerogram and posted them to Florio? He could not remember the reasons. *The function of the artist is to disturb. His duty is to arouse the sleepers . . .* The function of the nurse is to quiet the disturbed. Is every nurse an enemy to every artist?

Butch realizes he is losing his focus again. He knows he should get up and do something useful. He knows he should put himself to bed. But first he must do something about the box and its contents. He begins to put all of Florio's hidden life back into the box that holds secrets. He puts them back as carefully as a spy. He has been a spy. He locks the box and pushes it back under the bed under the dead-to-this-world weight of Florio. As he pushes, he keeps one eye on Florio's sleeping face. He does not want him to wake. He can't afford to let Florio find him snooping into the hidden life.

In his own bed on the camp cot he has set up near enough to Florio to be able to hear every cry he might make in the night, Butch asks himself what would have happened if Florio had awakened while the box was out and open? He does not know the answer. He does not know what rages or insights or forgiveness Florio can manage in his illness. Should he attempt to find out? Should he open the box again in the morning, drag it into the middle of the room, scatter photographs and diaries and poems every which way and rub Florio's eyes awake to it?

Florio ought to be made to look at the things that he has done to Evelyn and to Butch and to his other lovers and to himself in the pursuit of his art, shouldn't he? But even as Butch imagines doing this, he fluffs his thin pillow and slumps back into the thin mattress and wills himself to fall asleep as he hugs his teddy bear. But his will doesn't triumph. Something niggles. He knows there is something that he has quite forgotten to do. What? He rises from the cot and views the room by the light of the small lamp that is forever lit to hold back the total darkness that always terrifies him. His eyes pick out the old aerogram forgotten on the bedside table. Butch recovers it swiftly and squashes it into a tight ball and looks around for a place to throw it. And then he thinks again about this thing he has done and he rolls the ball of thin blue paper back and forth in the palm of his left hand with his thumb. What is he to do with Dr. Bethune's words? *The function of the artist is to disturb. His duty is to arouse the sleeper, to shake the complacent pillars* . . . Bethune's words re-emerge line by carefully printed line as the paper is unwadded and pressed flat against the surface of the table and smoothed out by Butch's fingers. Unwrinkled, the words are no longer quite so clear-cut as they were only moments ago. They no longer look nor read like the small incisions of a very sharp scalpel. In those early years in Montreal, Florio had used art like a sword. For the Florio of those days the only art that had mattered was the art that fought against British and American imperialism, the art that conserved realism and celebrated social solidarity. Florio had made his mark among the free egalitarian fraternity of Rue Ontario by denouncing American art in all its guises while promoting Canadian social realism in every guise he could unearth, including the naïve and primitive painters who lodged otherwise unappreciated in the boardinghouses of that quarter. And Florio had resisted the prevailing lies: popular culture was not going to save anybody from anything; new technologies were not going to make anything better for anybody.

Nobody in power offered Florio permanent teaching positions anywhere when his studies were over, and gallery owners dismissed his work. He struggled and Butch supported them by playing ragtime piano and boogie-woogie in a cocktail lounge and it was a life of sorts. Florio took occasional lovers, who drove trucks or worked with welding torches or plied the Seaway in iron and coke boats, and had a steadier girlfriend who taught English as a second language. Butch played jazz wherever and whenever he could and picked up hard rugged bodies of his own in bars. Florio sketched people on Rue St-Denis and then he painted what he'd sketched in the privacy of his studio. When he began, the people he painted were simple habitués of the street, students, hangers-on, revolutionaries. But a decade came and went and the revolutionaries grew older and became Péquistes and powerful, and Florio's portraits of their younger selves made it seem to them that Frederick Taylor — while still alive and retired in Mexico — had been reborn among them, and the workers Taylor had painted in the Angus shops of the thirties had given birth to the sons and daughters of the Paul Sauvé Arena of the mid-seventies.

Butch stares at Dr. Bethune's crumpled and straightened old words. *The function of the artist is to disturb. His duty is to arouse the sleepers, to shake the complacent pillars of the world. He reminds the world of its dark ancestry, shows the world its present, and points the way to its new birth* . . . But his thoughts have moved along to the words of another doctor, Florio's.

When Butch first arrived in the studio on The Main he had found Florio almost too weak to be moved from his bed. It was a scary shuffle to get him out of bed and down his stairs and into a taxi and up to the Royal Victoria's Emergency. Butch sat for three hours in a small, stuffy, overheated green room with no distraction other than a television set suspended overhead at a wrong angle to the chair upon which he sat clutching his overcoat and Florio's leather jacket against the company of other people as frightened as himself. He sat among the walking wounded of a premature Montreal winter and watched doctors and nurses who looked scarcely half his age come and go through a door that the public could not use. And he worried lest none of them would have the patience and tact to get to the bottom of Florio's illness.

He needn't have worried quite so much: the doctor who claimed Florio's dossier was their age, a man of experience, cultured enough to recognize Florio's paint-daubed clothing as an artist's working clothes, patient enough to probe Florio's psychological defence mechanisms and find an opening through which he could get the information he needed to diagnose something beyond common influenza. There was influenza but there was also malnutrition and stress and a kidney inflammation and insulin deficiency and more than adequate grounds for more testing than would be done in the normal course of events. As if to undercut the threat of this, to provide at least temporary reassurance, the doctor said, "Mr. Keller needs at least a couple of weeks in bed. He's worn out from too much work and not enough good food. He has viral and bacterial infections. I can prescribe something for them. He can't be admitted in his present condition unless there is no one to care for him at home. He has to be kept warm and quiet and well-fed to prevent pneumonia from developing."

Butch had done his best. Even so, fever had developed and then pneumonia and the doctor, bless him, had made a house call and taken further blood samples. Tomorrow, maybe, they'll hear from the doctor who will have heard from the lab. In the meantime, Florio sleeps.

7

Butch knows that Evelyn is at the heart of Florio's darkness. He knows that Evelyn has split Florio from his work. Evelyn has robbed Florio of his painterly gifts and left counterfeit coin behind. Butch knows that Florio cannot live without painting. Butch knows that Florio cannot really recover so long as his studio is home to all the neo-expressionist canvasses he has done of Evelyn. They exhaust him. They threaten to destroy him. It isn't just that they explode his reputation for lightness and clarity of composition. It isn't just that they deflect attention from the great strengths and true values in his more customary painterly concerns. It isn't just that they are an anomaly that defeats Butch every time he tries to compose his thoughts about them. Evelyn is dead, dead, dead. Butch feels her deathly presence in every nook and cranny in the studio, as if the twenty paintings stacked against the walls with Evelyn inside each and every one of them were a sort of nuclear furnace melting down Florio's life.

They leave him cold. Butch feels cold, ice cold. He rises from the camp cot and goes over to the paintings and turns them outwards towards him and lines them up

A Hole With A Head In It

along the wall. They are large canvasses and there is room for viewing only a few at a time.

The first three that he looks at, the last ones in the series in order of composition, remind Butch more than a little of the sort of thing Claude Breeze did in the sixties: *Lovers In A Landscape*. A man and a woman are flayed monsters of sexuality. The woman has been gored by a bull of a man. She is a matador dying but there is no bullring and no afternoon Spanish sunlight. The landscape is nowhere and nothing but sensuous abstraction. It is as near to abstract expressionism as Florio has ever gone. It is a great betrayal of the things that made his art honest and personal and sincerely felt.

Butch hates it and the ones to either side of it and all the others in the series enough to want to pick up the sharpest knife he can find and cut the canvasses to shreds. He wants to reduce them all to a heap of narrow ragged strips of canvas clotted with paint. He wants to kick apart the heavy wooden stretchers that hold the images taut against his consciousness. He wants to fall into a trance of vandalism and destroy Evelyn utterly in all the forms that Florio has given her. He wants to disinter all that remains of her inside Florio's box of souvenirs and make a fire of her. He wants to fall into a frenzy of violence against her until his arm grows so tired that he is merely hacking at her rather than slicing through her. He wants to burn her at the stake and reduce her to ashes after first drowning the life out of her like a common medieval witch. But he does nothing. There isn't a knife honed sharp enough to defeat her. There isn't a fire hot enough to destroy her. She is a poison against which there is no antidote. Butch knows that he can do nothing, nothing at all, against the death she brings.

Butch returns to his bed and tries to calms himself with thoughts of his mother. In his thoughts, she is always Mummy although Mummy does have a name. Mummy's name is Estelle Mary Grant Benet. Benet was her erstwhile husband, Butch's father, but he is long forgotten and his name remains only because Mummy has never surrendered anything she has been given. Butch does not know much about him, only the little that Mummy has told him and this is truly very little. Mummy has always told him a great many too many things about altogether too many people in whom Butch has not had the slightest interest. His mother has spoken of his father rarely and always in this dismissive way: "I could never trust your father for a moment in the company of other women. He was a womanizer of the worst sort." She has never told him what a better sort of womanizer might be like.

Butch finds it easy to think about Mummy. Mummy is inescapable. She is always there, just at the edge of consciousness, right at the centre of emotional response. If Florio was to wake up, he thinks, and smile and say, Butch, a penny for your thoughts, he would say, You're a spendthrift, Florio, I wasn't thinking about anything at all. He would say this because he doesn't like talking to Florio about Mummy. It's too disloyal. He cannot quite say why. But it doesn't matter. Not here. Not now. Florio isn't awake and he never smiles in his sleep and he'd never say anything so conventional as, A penny for your thoughts. So Butch is left to talk to the teddy bear that he has brought with him to Montreal. Butch likes to talk to Teddy about his mother as if he was talking to a stranger on a train or to a sleeping lover whose name he can't quite remember. It is only to perfect strangers and to sleeping lovers and to Teddy that he can say, I think most mothers must resent their sons at least some of the time and I guess that there are some mothers who resent their sons most of the time, but honestly, I sometimes think Mummy resents me all of the time. You know I try not to take this personally any more, not, at least, too personally. Mummy has been badly used by men. Mummy has been abused by recent history but women like her have taught people like me where to take a stand with the men in our lives. We owe them something for their pains.

In bed, into his old and nearly threadbare teddy, he whispers, "I've read Marx too. I'm not a dumb fucking machine. I looked at Mummy's life and I learned how to use the dialectic of history to my own advantage. Mummy is nearly seventy but she stopped counting years and years ago. She's just fiftyish. Even so she expects me to remember her birthday. Always. Every August twenty-second, Mummy expects me to bring her flowers and a bottle of good champagne, some scent or something in silk from Holt's and a chocolate cake that I've baked myself. She doesn't expect a card and she doesn't want me to wish her a Happy Birthday but she does want her chocolate cake and I have to have baked it myself or there's a flood. She expects all this even though she knows that her birthday is on the same date as Florio's. The last time she went into flood was last Christmas, you remember, Teddy, I forgot to order her a poinsettia. I had to run out and pick one up at a florist's just before closing time. It was a wretched thing. Mummy went on and on about it and I got angry and pitched it right into the garbage. She didn't mind that very much. But then I went and called her Mother instead of Mummy and she flooded again and stopped speaking to me until January sixth. Epiphany is a major feast in her books. She forgives everyone everything on the day that the Three Wise Men brought gold, frankincense and myrrh to the stable in Bethlehem. It's an old custom left over from her childhood. I don't understand it although it was supposed to be a part of my childhood too.

"I've grown up but Mummy has only ever grown old. Have you noticed how Catholics never think they're the least bit superstitious? They'll tell you that there's nothing the least bit irrational in their religion. So they're suckers for astrology. Mummy regards herself as a gifted astrologer. She casts her own horoscopes. She's a Sun in Leo on the cusp of Virgo with her moon in Libra with Cancer rising. This, she says, means that she's frank, open-hearted, generous and has a marked dramatic flair. These signs, she says, make her a sincere and affectionate lover who is highly appreciative of affection freely returned. The planets that rule her, she says, attract her most and make her most attractive to refined and harmonious people who join her in easy alliances. These same planets, she says, have given her a hatred of small details and a preference for doing things in a big way. These planets, she says, make her quick to anger but just as quick to forgive. These planets, she says, have given her strong interests in food and hygiene, a liking for very good clothes and a dependence upon the accomplishments of her child. These are the things Mummy has been telling her friends year after year after year. Some of her friends have come to believe her. Some of her friends think she's a gifted psychic. I keep trying to tell her that everything she says of herself must also apply to Florio. They have more than the same birthdays, they do have all the same signs. But she just ignores what I say about him, I mean about the things I say in his favour. Me, I'm a Sun in Scorpio with Moon in Virgo on the cusp of Sagittarius with Capricorn rising. This makes me suspicious, sceptical, critical, reserved and calculating. I'm forceful, blunt and sarcastic, courageous, bold, daring. There's a love of the elemental in me and a fascination with the sea, Teddy, isn't there?"

Butch looks at Florio asleep and promises the teddy bear he has carried everywhere with him since boarding school days that if it is truly time for Florio to die, that if the disease within him is a killer, his ashes will be dropped in the sea on the shore of Mahone Bay where the ashes of Evelyn and the stillborn child now rest. Until then, he will go to sleep remembering the old cowboy song that used to be a joke between them in the dormitory just before the lights went out —

> *Oh, I sometimes think I'm locoed*
> *and just fit for counting sheep*
> *'Cause I only think of you*
> *When I'm waking or asleep.*

> *I'm wearing Cupids hobbles*
> *And I'm tied to Love's stake-pin,*
> *Cause when my heart was branded*
> *Your iron sunk right in*

— and press Teddy tight against his chest.

WILLIAM BURROUGHS IN WESTMOUNT

William Powell Blazer is sitting in a new black Jeep Cherokee parked outside an undistinguished red brick rowhouse in the middle part of Westmount on a Saturday morning in April. He is waiting for his son to emerge from the house. His son is not ready on time. This is no accident. There are no accidents in his relations with Sonja, his son's mother. He is taught again and again what will happen if he falls behind in his child support payments. Get up that money or no son. He was a couple of days late this month. His son has been late every Saturday since then. Sonja is a monopolist — she never gives anything away for nothing, never gives more than she has to give, always takes as much back as she possibly can. While he waits, he does not wonder about this. He wonders about William Burroughs.

Now William Powell Blazer is almost exactly the kind of man his name suggests: he is well-groomed, clean shaven except for a well-trimmed moustache, only ever so slightly informal, nicely set-up, manicured. He has almost nothing of the beat-up or the beatnik about him except that he is dressed in jeans, T-shirt and black leather jacket, but even these he wears in a safe, pressed way, less rakishly than, say, Bryan Adams. His morals are a little less neatly packaged than his manner but are certainly not outlaw: William Powell Blazer earns his living easily as a real estate agent who specializes in selling commercial buildings to overseas investors who sometimes arrive at his office with briefcases brimming with worn American currency and always insist upon seeing a notary and becoming Québec Numbered Companies before leaving. And William Powell Blazer is not a junkie: he's late thirtysomething and like most of this generation he has tried cocaine and an assortment of other recreational drugs, but he is not now and never has been addicted to any controlled substance. So why is he daydreaming about William Burroughs — beatnik, outlaw, junkie — while Sonja monopolizes more of his time than she is owed?

William Powell Blazer is thinking about the notorious author of *Naked Lunch* because Gabrielle, the woman for whom he left Sonja but with whom he is not yet cohabiting, has invited him to attend a vernissage of William Burroughs's paintings later this same Saturday. Despite Gabrielle's assurances that the aged Godfather of the Beat Generation is going to attend the vernissage in person and is fabulously interesting and entertaining to see, to hear, to meet, he isn't convinced that the exhibit is something he wants to be seen seeing. These days William Powell Blazer is very circumspect about his public image, and the images that Gabrielle conjured up don't seem quite suited to the one he wants to project before the judge at the next hearing of his petition for joint custody of his son. Even so, the idea of meeting William Burroughs is fascinating. He doesn't know much about him but he does know that Burroughs is not his kind of person. This is enough. He is tired of his kind of people. He is tired of the kind of person he was when he was married to Sonja. And so, in his daydream, he imagines himself just *hanging out* with William Burroughs even though he is not quite sure what this means beyond *not* doing certain uncool things, such as getting embarrassed in Gabrielle's bedroom. It is a very fuzzy fantasy.

The black door of the house opens and a small white-haired boy emerges through the white-painted front porch and half-slides down the black iron stair railing and walks dreamily to the curb. "Did you kiss your Mummy goodbye and tell her that you're leaving? I'm not getting out, Willy," William Powell Blazer tells his son, William Powell Blazer, Junior.

The small boy climbs up and inside the black Cherokee and nestles down into the white leather upholstery of the front bucket seat and buckles his black nylon seat belt across his chest slowly but without adult assistance.

"It's okay, Dad. I already kissed her. Pat can see me from the window and she'll tell Mummy when I'm gone," his son says with the assurance of a five-year-old that the world needs no more kisses than he has already given it and will watch over him safely in return. He eyes his son warily. The spontaneous affection that once existed between them has given way to a dry manner tinged with suspicion on both sides. He can feel the heat rising on his neck. His face swells and his lips turn purple. He wants to demand *Where is your mother for Christ's sake and why isn't she waving you goodbye?* Instead, he asks "Who is this Pat?"

"Pat slept over last night. We had lots of fun. We made popcorn. We listened to Beatles records. We danced. It was great. I had some beer," the boy says sincerely.

He checks the snugness of the child's seat belt. He puts the car in gear and begins the sharp descent into the lower reaches of Westmount. The trees sweeping all the way down the mountainside to the railway lines are still winter-bleached. Spring will not come early this year. "It certainly sounds like you had a great time," he replies with a face-saving irony not as far beyond his son's comprehension as he thinks it is. "I don't know Pat, do I?"

"Pat is just a friend of Mummy's from the Y. Can we go to McDonald's for lunch, Dad? I have my own money. Pat gave me five dollars!"

He wants to cry out, *Why is she bribing you? What is it that you are not supposed to tell me under any condition?* But as one judge said to another, Be just, and if you can't be just, be arbitrary. He says, "You'll have to give it back to her."

"No! It's mine! Pat says I can keep it! Pat says it's in case I have a Big Mac attack when she's not around! Last time you said we could go to McDonald's next time! Remember? This is next time, isn't it, Dad? Huh?"

"Tell me about Pat and we'll see."

"Oh, Daddy! She's just this lady who sits with me sometimes when Mummy has to go out somewhere. She tells me stories about the Beatles. She met John Lennon once but he wasn't a Beatle any more. He was wearing a white suit and no shoes and he was very clean. I didn't have to put on my slippers after she gave me my bath. Pat drinks beer. She gave me some beer to drink and then I went to bed. She smokes too. She can blow smoke rings! I saw her do it when I got up to have a pee-pee. She said I didn't know how to hold my beer but that was a joke I think."

"I think so too. And she slept over last night?" he asks more edgily than he intended. His nerves are getting to be a social liability even with his son.

"She slept in Mummy's bed, Dad! I know because I thought I was hugging Mummy when I climbed in this morning."

"You mean she slept with your Mummy?" *Your honour, my wife is openly having an affair with another woman right in front of Willy's eyes.* He asks himself if there's anything he won't say to stop the past from invading the present, to get her dead air out of his lungs? Probably not.

"Mummy didn't come home till after breakfast. I saw her come home in a taxi! I wasn't watching for her. I wasn't afraid. She said she wasn't going to come home till morning so I wasn't worried about her. I just forgot about it when I was asleep but Pat let me hug her. Then me and Pat watched cartoons. Pat likes cartoons too."

"I bet she does," William says mindlessly. He is working hard assimilating the new data his son has fed him. No one he knows ever tells him anything about his estranged wife unless he digs it out. Is Sonja dating? She must be dating. Who could she be seeing? Not another woman, not her, not really. Is it anyone he knows? How can he find out? "Where did Mummy go last night?"

"I forget," the small boy says glumly.

"That's okay, sport, maybe you'll remember before we get to McDonald's."

"Are we going to McDonald's? Are we really going, Daddy?"

"We have to get you registered for T-ball first, sport. Whatever that is."

"It's a game!"

"Well, I had guessed that!"

While Willy gives him an overly elaborate description of T-ball, a game that he soon realizes is no more than a small-fry version of baseball, he runs down a mental list of the guys he knows who always wanted to bop Sonja. Who is the likeliest to be doing it now that he is out of the picture? Coming to no reasonable conclusion nor even to a fascinatingly irrational one, he turns his head to the matter more immediately at hand and looks for a parking space on the library side of Westmount Park. He's thinking it would be pleasant to walk with his son across the park to the arena but the parking lot is already filled with new white Lincoln Town cars and vintage white Rollers and '60s Caddies that have been rented by the wedding parties now being photographed in the Victorian greenhouse. It revives a memory of his own wedding, a black and white wedding, a very traditional Presbyterian wedding, full of formality, tails and boiled shirtfronts, lobsters, white wine and firm handshakes, lovely to look at on video. So his mother says. He'll take her word for it. His mother also says that he and Sonja must settle their differences, get together again, rebuild Willy's shattered world. She won't accept his word that all that is now impossible and that Willy feels torn, not shattered. If his mother knew who was bopping Sonja, she would tell him. She'd go further. She'd phone the other guy's mother and tell her to tell her son to leave her grandson's mother alone. And they would do as they'd been told. His mother is like a vampire bat. She secretes a narcotic effluvium that anesthetizes everyone within listening range and renders them harmless. And then she'd call him back and say *Your father and I had our differences too but we always managed to work them out. Spend a little of your capital. Invest in your marriage. Buy Sonja something beautiful for the house. She'll appreciate it. I know I always did.* His father was her primary victim. His father had a shiny red face and little piggy eyes that lit up when he looked at women and went out when he looked at his son. Burroughs's paintings are accidental, abstract, impressionistic, Gabrielle has said. Not the kind of thing his mother would have in mind.

Around on the arena side, the parking situation is no better: there is a tremendous crush of cars and people outside the hockey rink. He zigs and zags through congested traffic on Park Place and out into the neighbouring streets while his son continues to find things to say about T-ball. Not spotting a place to park the Cherokee legally, he doubles back and puts it in the bus stop facing the hockey arena on St. Catherine Street as his son describes how you have to touch home plate in order to score a run. Opening his door, sniffing at the April air, he remembers when this stretch of St. Catherine always used to smell of baking bread, as homely as his grandmother's kitchen, but that was in the days before the bricks and red Spanish roof tiles of Harrison's bakery had become the facade of a bulky white-stuccoed condominium. He wonders what good smells his son will remember when he grows up. Sonja's kitchen always smells of rotting vegetables, mouldy fruit and cats. His own mother's kitchen always smells of disinfectant. St. Catherine smells of dog shit. He holds his son's hand tightly as they cross the road and wishes that he could still carry him to safety everywhere, but the kid plays T-ball now, walks like a man, lives with Sonja, looks sincere all the time.

As they approach the low brick building, they fall into step alongside Vergil and Winston Lane. Winston is one of Willy's classmates.

"Hi guys," Vergil says and ruffles the small boy's white hair with a big black hand. "How you doing?"

William Powell Blazer shrugs as he looks at Vergil's

bright wide white toothy smile. He feels suddenly aggrieved that all the brightest smiles and the whitest names he has been dealing with lately go with brown or black faces. Vergil is a very dark-skinned Barbadian documentary filmmaker married to a strawberry blonde who went to Trafalgar School For Girls with Sonja's younger sister. Winston's skin is the colour of café au lait. As Vergil continues to smile happily, his feeling of aggravation deepens. Vergil, he tells himself, has every right to have married a classic Westmount beauty with money and to have fathered a wonderful child and to be happy with his family. But how did he do it? Magic, taboos, spells, amulets, voodoo dolls? How did he get her to loosen up, unfreeze? There is something very remarkable in this. *I'm not a racist!* he tells himself. *I'm just curious, jealous, indignant, pissed off.* His aggravation with Vergil is pure envy. He'd like to know the secret of voodoo. Instead, he asks, "Vergil, you're a literary sort. What should a guy like me know about William Burroughs?"

"What would you like to know about him?"

"Enough to get me through cocktails."

"Most people only know him for *Naked Lunch*, so you don't have to pretend to have read anything more than that. Have you read it?"

"No. I can't say that I have."

"Well, that doesn't matter very much either. You can say that you found it a trifle too disturbing. Disturbing — not disgusting. Disgust might put you in company you don't want to be with but everyone is allowed to be disturbed by Burroughs. He attacks the nerves — that's his strength. He's not really a pornographer — sex is incidental to his work. The dirtiest bits of *Naked Lunch* are parts of a Swiftian satire against hanging. Its main thrust is the depiction of lust in all its forms. His junkies are models for the human condition because they are creatures of total need and hence of total vulnerability. Morally, he's as austere as any Puritan. Will that do?"

"I don't know if they'll be talking about his books.

People are going to be there to look at his paintings. Am I allowed to smile when I'm introduced to him?"

"Burroughs will be at this party, will he? You're moving in very different company these days, William. I'm impressed. Yes, smile by all means. Even laugh. He's a bit of a humorist in the fashion of Mark Twain. I didn't know he was a painter."

"I don't know that it's such a big deal — my meeting him." He sniffles and then clears his throat into his handkerchief. He inspects the phlegm, which is flecked with blood. "Yuck!"

"What's the matter?" Vergil asks benignly.

"I've got a bad taste in my mouth. Bleeding sinuses. It's going to take us hours to get in and registered and out again. I don't know if I have the patience for all that this morning. It's too nice a day and I don't get much time with Willy. I think I'll take him out for an adventure and let his mother bring him another time."

"I think you'll find this is the only registration they're going to have," Vergil responds softly. "But I don't think all these people have come to register their children for T-ball. Some are here for the gun show."

"Can't we stay, please, Daddy? I don't want to miss this. I want to be on Winston's team."

"The what show?" He resists the tug of his son's hand against his own.

Vergil points to a poster taped to a nearby lamppost. It's illustrated with a nice drawing of an old revolver and announces that a show and sale of guns, knives and other memorabilia is being held inside the arena and that the price of admission is four dollars.

"You're feeling bad, William, you don't need to stand in line with a bunch of kids, I can register both the boys and see you outside," Vergil says slowly, wary of giving offence.

His face lightens. Gabrielle has told him that William Burroughs is obsessed with firearms. He used to know a lot about guns. He figures that if he can do a quick study of some of these, recover old knowledge, maybe he won't have to say anything about books he hasn't read or paintings that won't mean much. It's a thought. "That's nice of you, Vergil. Sonja will nail another piece of me to her lawyer's desk if I take Willy with me but I'll stay with the boys if you want to have a look first."

"I'm not eager to step into a room full of white guys and guns," Vergil says half-smiling. "You go ahead."

"Is this okay with you, Willy? Will you stay here with Winston?" His son doesn't hear the question or maybe just doesn't think any answer is required: his white head is bowed alongside Winston's curly black one over the packs of hockey cards both boys have squirreled out of their pants pockets.

A lady at a card table in the foyer takes his money and stamps a red star on the back of his left hand. "You can go in and out as many times as you want without paying again," she explains, "as long as you don't wash your hand."

As he steps out of the April sunshine in the foyer into the fluorescent illumination of the hockey rink and sets foot on the cold, grey, damp concrete floor where artificial ice has lain all winter, he enters a world that is surprisingly matter-of-fact. The rows of trestle tables running two-thirds the length of the rink are separated by wide aisles filled with groups of people moving raggedly in both directions as they inspect the displays arranged on the tables. A cafeteria is set up at the far end and a smell of strong coffee mixes with the scent of machine oil. But then he notices something distinctly different: it's an old-fashioned male gathering. There are some women around but they are outnumbered ten or twelve to one by guys. He stands a little straighter, sucks in his stomach a notch more, thrusts out his chest and begins to take an unself-conscious interest in the things on display.

A ragged-ass boy in a dirty Expos cap and out-at-the-knee jeans is running his finger along the outside edge of a glass case containing a dozen police handguns that are being exhibited with a sign saying Please Do Not Handle

Without Permission. A retired British Army type in a threadbare blazer and crumpled plaid golf slacks is har-har-ing loudly with a timid little man behind the display table. But within seconds, William is overwhelmed by the oddness of it all. Here, enclosed in a few square yards of Westmount, is an arsenal large enough to wage a revolution against all of Québec. However, the people are not revolutionaries half-mad with blood lust. There are guys dressed like mobsters and there are guys dressed like bikers and there are guys dressed like gentlemen farmers and there are guys dressed like cowboys and there are guys dressed like frontiersmen and there are guys dressed like cops, but the only psychological state all these guys have in common is a love of costume. Otherwise, they look and talk like everyday shoppers at a flea market. Canny shoppers. They aren't greedy for the guns. In fact, they seem mildly uninterested in them. If they have eyes for anything, it is uniforms. There are racks and racks of uniforms from every war in which America was involved. The stuff from Viet Nam is mobbed by others but scares him to death — it is too high-tech, fatal. He shudders and passes by, stopping next at a stall displaying Nazi insignia as theatrical as movie props. Held in hand, looked at closely, the flags, uniforms and medals startle by the quality of the workmanship. He has never before realized that the symbols carried and worn by the people who trampled down the Jewish spirit and body in the Holocaust had been tailored and crafted so expertly by such skilled hands, probably Jewish hands. He admires an enamelled double eagle on a silver brooch, is tempted to buy it but thinks better of it. Some people might not understand. *Your honour, I am not a fascist! I didn't buy it for its symbolism!*

"Hey man, come over here."

He abruptly stops admiring the Nazi officer's insignia and looks up guiltily.

Two guys in black T-shirts emblazoned with Harley-Davidson logos who look like real heavy-duty bikers wave him over to their table. All it displays are a few matchboxes and a bone-handled knife. They are insistent. "Hey man, yeah, you, come over here."

He doesn't feel he can walk away without creating a disturbance so he goes over and stands stiffly and listens as one biker explains that the matchboxes contain a kind of precision screw that can be attached to the blade of any jackknife in such a way as to allow the blade to be opened with a flick of the thumb. William Powell Blazer stands stiffer than a ramrod while the other biker demonstrates this amazing invention a few inches from his belly on a knife that seems to have been designed for disembowelling black bears.

"Hey man, it's yours for twenty bucks."

"I don't have a knife."

"We got a pal over there sells knives. He'll fix you up, then come back here and see us."

He laughs, the biker speaks so earnestly. The biker shrugs it off. "Shit, man, you better get one. Don't you read the newspaper? There are all sorts of weird guys out there kill you for twenty dollars while you're waiting for the bus. We got to take care of ourselves, man. You can't trust the cops to take care of business. No way. Get a knife."

As he roams the rest of the display area steering clear of the bikers, he keeps being drawn back to one display. It features guns of the American West. Within a hundred square feet, a dealer has enclosed multiple examples of the guns that once fuelled his imagination. Growing up in the heyday of television Westerns, he had been obsessed by the things men had used to kill one another in frontier gunfights. Instead of collecting hockey cards, he had amassed a thick wad of cards illustrating the history of rifles and handguns and had traded them until he possessed everything relating to the Colt, Winchester and Remington arms companies. These had been his favourites, his Oilers and Penguins and Flames. And here they are — the real thing — a rack of commemorative edition Winchester 73s, gilded, embossed, engraved and blued; a brace of .44 Ned Buntline Specials with carved ivory handgrips and twelve-inch silvered barrels in a velvet-lined presentation case; a table of Remington and Colt Lightnings, Thunderers, Peacemakers, Armys, Navys, Riders, Derringers, Theurs, Roots, Walkers and Dragoons chained together. He wants to touch them but can't. He feels too shy. These are things that the heroes of his childhood owned. The sense of their past glory reduces him to his childish self, makes him as vagrant as a penniless kid in a candy store.

To avoid being accosted by the dealer, who looks as if, like a used car salesman, he knows the price of everything and the value of nothing, he wanders over to another stall where a man is selling air pistols. There are a couple of Daisy handguns that look like Nazi sidearms and fire a dozen BBs in a burst. They are quite interesting but the thing that captivates him is a pellet pistol that looks like a cowboy revolver. The salesman says, "Now this, friend, is a near-perfect replica of a Colt Peacemaker. It has tremendous firepower and you don't need a licence to own it. I can let you have it for a hundred dollars. It's a demonstrator. Here, try it in your hand. Feels like a feather, doesn't it? That's perfect balance for you."

He holds it and it feels weightless, a simple extension of his arm. *You want peace, Sonja, here — have a piece of my Peacemaker* and he looks into her death-dealing, reptilian eyes, eyes without a trace of warmth or lust or hate or any feeling for him beyond monopolistic greed — cold, intense, impersonal, predatory. *This will last a lifetime.* "How do you load it?" he asks tentatively.

The salesman shows him how to insert the compressed air cylinder and how to load the five firing chambers with pellets, and then hands it over in a brown paper bag with a tin of ammunition in exchange for two fifty dollar bills that William peels off a roll of cash he jams back in his jeans pocket.

"Have yourself some fun, friend."

Outside Vergil and the boys are waiting for him. Willy for once isn't Sonja's son and doesn't ask him what he has in the bag. Willy is too excited by various things Winston has proposed they do and Willy is afraid he will dash these ideas unless they are shouted out all at once. Whatever the boy wants to do, it's okay with him. He has just done something he has never done before: he has bought himself a gun. It makes him feel right and bright. Pure perfect pleasure rushes to his head. Electricity through his brain like a line of coke. He's so connected to pleasure that he casually accepts a parking ticket from the Public Security Officer who is writing it out just as they return to the Cherokee.

"Aren't you going to holler at him?" Willy asks.

"Not this time," he says. *Your honour, I am changing. Ask my son what happened when I got a parking ticket last Saturday!* He exhales expansively, "So where exactly is it that we're going now?"

"McDonald's! But can we get some more hockey cards first?" Willy shouts.

The Lanes have not brought a car so he taxis them on a side trip to a shop that sells the full range — Topps, O-Pee-Chee, ProSet, Score, Upper Deck — and then on the main trip to McDonald's. He tries to tell Vergil about the gun show and how ordinary and harmless it seemed to have all those guns just lying there but he can't get the point across. Vergil is not willing to concede that guns can ever be harmless. So he gives up and they just listen to the two boys trade their new hockey cards. For lunch, he buys everyone what they want except himself because he really doesn't want to eat anything on offer and orders a coffee just to be polite. On the way back to the Cherokee, they pass a sports store and he goes in and buys a ball and a plastic bat. Back at the park, they bat the ball back and forth and Vergil talks about what a fine game cricket is until everybody has had enough. Then Winston says he and Willy want to watch movies the rest of the afternoon.

At the video shop on Victoria Avenue, while the two boys try to decide between *An American Tale*, which they've both seen twice, and *A Hard Day's Night*, which Willy sees every time he has the chance, and while Vergil engages in an arcane debate about horror films with the young guy behind the counter, William looks out the window and watches people pass by. A moment later, he half-wishes he had been looking elsewhere, because he sees Gabrielle and she sees him and he is drawn to her like a moth to its mate in a haze of horniness. He glides out the door and sidles up to her on the sidewalk. "Surprised to see me here?"

"I thought you were with your son."

"He's inside. Getting a video with a friend. What have you been doing?"

"I've been shopping. Lingerie. Do you want to see?"

"In the street?"

"My place. In an hour."

"Ten minutes."

"What about your son?"

"He's seen enough of me. All he wants to do now is watch movies with his friend. I've seen the movies."

"Are you sure?"

"Ten minutes."

Back in the video store, he reaches for his roll of cash and strips off a twenty-dollar bill. "The videos are on me," he says scrunching it into Vergil's shirt pocket, "and something to send him home in a cab with when you've had enough of his company. I wish I could hang around and watch the films with you but if I don't get some groceries now, I starve next week. If you can't get him home by five, just phone his mother. She doesn't seem to mind what he does as long as he doesn't do it with me." William kisses Willy hurriedly. "Sorry I can't hang out with you guys anymore today but maybe next Saturday. Ask Mummy, okay." And then he's out the door before any objections can be raised.

Ten minutes later, he's down the street and around the corner and down the road and up a hundred feet above St. Catherine Street ringing the buzzer of the condo where Gabrielle is living just now.

"You were fast. I just got through the door myself," she says.

Gabrielle is in the real estate game too but she sells residential properties that have fizzled for other agents. She makes them sizzle by adding special touches — fresh flower arrangements, small oriental carpets, striking artwork, the smell of fresh cinnamon in the kitchen, and her own live-in presence if the owners are out of town. She puts him on broil with a kiss that goes all the way to the back of his throat and a hand that goes all the way down the front of his pants. "I bought some very nice things," she says. "Pour yourself a vodka while I put them on."

He doesn't ask her if she wants one. She doesn't need Dutch courage like he does. While he sips from a leaded crystal glass she has left out on the sideboard, his eyes sweep the room, hesitate at the most strategic points — the fireplace, the ends and front of the sofa, the visible wall of the dining alcove. Gabrielle has added bold colours to the earth tones of the owners — splashes of gold, reds, purples highlighted by the purest of whites. Two large squares of white silk lie on the sidechair next to the telephone table. They catch his eye.

"In case you're wondering what to do with the scarves," she calls through from the bedroom, "put one on and hold the other and then let me see you."

He folds one scarf into a triangle and ties it below his eyes so that it covers the lower half of his face like an outlaw or maybe just a vigilante. The other he rolls into a rope that he flexes between his two hands. He does this without thinking too much about what he is doing. With Gabrielle, he must act without hesitation.

At the bedroom door, he sees her reflection in the full-length dressmaker's mirror beside the bed. Her back is to him and her body from small bust to ample hips is cinched into a red satin corselette trimmed with gold lace. Below it, a golden garter belt supports white silk stockings drawn smooth over her shapely legs. She is slightly bent from the waist, her buttocks flared. As she straightens, she turns and he encounters a double view of her in the mirror and in the room. She puts her hands to her face in a theatrical gesture of alarm and asks "Who are you?"

He says, "Don't make any noise and do exactly as I say and I won't hurt you." He says the words slowly, flatly, almost reassuringly, as she has taught him to say them.

"You'll have to tie my hands behind my back or I'll scratch your eyes out," she says just as he expects her to say it. It is a scene they play out in various costumes but always with the same script.

He pushes her backwards roughly against the bed and jerks her over on to her belly. He twists her hands behind her and ties them loosely with the scarf. He says once more, "Don't make any noise and do exactly as I say and I won't hurt you." As he presses her against the purple satin bedspread, he forces her legs open and unzips his jeans. And he doesn't hurt her and she doesn't say anything.

Fifteen minutes later, he unties her hands and retreats to the kitchen where he makes a pot of herbal tea to the sounds of water splashing in the bathroom. Gabrielle is wrapped in a red Chinese silk kimono when she joins him at the kitchen table for her tisane. She says, "That worked for me. Was it okay for you?"

It is what he expects her to say. He goes, "Ummmm." It is what she expects of him when they have sex this way.

Then she says, "I bought you a little something today. But before I give them to you, you must promise to wear them when we go to see Burroughs tonight."

The prospect of a present ends his indecision about going to the vernissage. She is forever buying him presents and he is forever grateful for them. Her presents — his black leather jacket among them — always reassure him that she truly appreciates the things he does for her. But, even more than this, they nudge him further away from his life with Sonja.

William Burroughs in Westmount

In the larger of the two gift-wrapped boxes she produces from the sideboard he finds a pair of lizardskin cowboy boots — dark brown and intricately patterned by nature. In the smaller of the boxes, almost weightless, is a bottle-green silk shirt. Between them, the two presents probably cost her a thousand dollars and not a second thought. Gabrielle is careless about money. When she has it, she spends it. When she's broke, she goes without everything and accepts nothing from him, survives on the jewellery she pawns. It's an imbalance he'd like to correct. When she moves out of here next week, he wants her to move in with him.

"Put the boots on. Do they fit?" she asks eagerly.

He pulls against the stiff leather until his feet hit bottom. He stands up, rocks back and forth on his heels, walks around the room. "They're wonderful. They take a little getting used to because of the heel height. I think I'll keep them on, break them in. Now, about tonight, tell me what I'm supposed to expect."

"Here, I'll read you something from *Naked Lunch*. It's his most famous book."

He is waiting in front of the scuffed white elevator doors in the parking garage of his building. He is listening for the sounds of the elevator's descent. The cage has stopped a couple of floors up and seems stalled there. A light coughing alerts him. Two young guys, one white, the other black, step out of the shadows at the left edge of his vision. His neck hairs stand on end. He is very vulnerable, his arms full — groceries, Gabrielle's shirt, his sneakers, the pellet gun. These guys are looking at him with the neutral, calm glance of animals. Like all hunters, they size up their prey before striking. The elevator isn't moving. He turns to face them. He sees they're grey-skinned, drooling, yellow-eyed, shabbily dressed. The black guy is wearing a badly stained jogging suit. The white guy has baggy-assed jeans, a checked shirt, a baseball cap on backwards. They both smell sickly sweet — dried urine, old sweat, something else. Junk food? Junkies? He feels his blood rushing through him like a locomotive.

"You want something?" he asks, less than neutrally.

"Yeah. You got a light?"

"You're kidding, right?"

"Yeah, right, man, you got money. We want it."

"Sorry, guys, the grocery guy got to me first."

"Don't shit us, man. We seen you at the rink. You got money. We want it. You got a watch, rings, credit cards, we take that too," the white guy says, slurring the words.

"Else you get our knives, motherfucker," the black guy adds. They look at one another and grin with satisfaction at the terror they think they're inspiring. In that moment of inattention, he curves his back and braces his right foot against the elevator door.

"Start moving for that money, motherfucker. You don't think we got knives? Show the man your knife, short stuff."

He pushes himself off the door with his right foot, hurtling forward, crashing into them with all his parcels, dropping the bags as he bumps them. He is past them and wheeling around and running back at them sprawled on the concrete floor and kicking the black guy in the small of the back and bringing both hands locked together over the head and around the neck of the white guy and squeezing hard and slamming his face into the cindercrete wall, releasing him and screaming at the black guy who is finding his feet, "Get the fuck out of here, now, junkie!" He finds his parcel with the pellet gun in it at his feet, picks the Peacemaker up and holds it to the head of the white guy. "You too, shitface queer!"

They do as he says — very quickly.

By the time the elevator finally reaches the parking level, he has his groceries roughly bagged and back in his arms. He holds them tight against him, careless of the contents, and rests against the wall as the cage rises to his floor. He thinks about mugwumps.

Whenever he has thought about mugwumps in the

William Burroughs in Westmount

past, he has had people like his father and his father's father and their friends in mind — big time fence sitters, ideological anythingarians, bosses of small-bore politicians, the wheeler-dealer financial manipulators of Westmount, Québec, Canada. But now he sees mugwumps sitting naked on stools covered in pink silk sucking translucent syrups through alabaster straws and licking honey from crystal goblets. They have thin, purple-blue lips, long black tongues, razor-sharp beaks of black bone. He knows that in times of panic, mugwumps take refuge in walls and remain there for weeks in biostasis.

Fishing the keys out of his back pocket with thumb and forefinger without unburdening himself, he fumbles around until he unlocks his door. Pushing it open with his back, he enters his apartment slowly, carefully. Mugwumps flee his mind, stash themselves in his walls.

After they'd finished the tisane, Gabrielle went with him to get his groceries at Cinq Saisons. While they'd waited for the butcher to finish trimming the veal scallopini, Gabrielle explained that William Burroughs makes paintings by setting cans of spray paint in front of plywood panels and exploding the cans with bullets shot from an assortment of guns. Real bullets. Real guns. The results, she said, were fabulously interesting. What Burroughs does to make a painting, he thinks, must be against the law. A man can't just shoot up things, not even in the privacy of his own home, can he? He stands in the entranceway considering the legality of this long enough for a thin red juice to begin leaking through the bags of groceries onto his brand new boots.

He has one hell of a blinding pain in his gut.

He feels light-headed.

He is afraid to let go of his parcels and look at his stomach.

He thinks he saw, then felt the white guy's knife flash in the darkness of the basement as he hurtled past them.

What he did to save a few bucks, he thinks, must be against the law. A man can't just beat up junkies, not even in the privacy of his own garage, can he? He considers the legality of this.

His telephone begins to ring. He really ought to do something about it. He does not know what to do about it. A mugwump is watching him from behind the hall mirror. Its eyes — blank as obsidian mirrors, pools of black blood, glory holes in a toilet wall — follow him into the kitchen. He places his bags carefully on the counter and leans against them. His telephone is connected to an answering machine and he hears the machine click into action and record the incoming message.

Wavering beside a growing pool of thin red juice that may be from nothing more than the broken packet of veal scallopini, he hears his ex-wife say "William, it's me, Sonja. Are you there? Are you listening? I hope you're listening so that you won't be able to just erase what I have to say when you get home. What the hell game are you playing? You take me to court because you think you're not seeing enough of your son and that I don't know how to raise him properly on my own. So I let you see more of him than we had agreed to when you left me for your whore and what do you do? You give him twenty bucks and leave him all afternoon with people we hardly know who really aren't our kind of people at all. Does this make sense? I really don't understand. What is it that you want? Do you have any bloody idea what you want? I mean beyond driving me crazy. I've got a lot more to say to you but I don't feel like wasting my breath right now. I will tell you one last thing, though. Do you want to know what your son asked me when he came home? He asked me if he could change his name. He doesn't want his name to be the same as yours. So I asked him if he'd like it better if we started calling him 'Billy' and do you know what he said? He said 'Let's call Daddy that instead.' I think he has a point. At the rate things are going, he's going to grow up before you ever do. Think about it, Billy. Billy the Kid."

There's silence and then the machine clicks and flashes a red number one. His face is drained of blood. He

William Burroughs in Westmount

does not like hearing Sonja's voice in his own apartment. Sonja is a monopolist — she never gives anything away for nothing, never gives more than she has to give, always takes as much back as she possibly can. He has trouble understanding this. He has trouble understanding many things. Its the after-effect of adrenalin. It isn't at all clear to him why he did what he did down in the garage a few minutes ago. He knows how he did it. Adrenalin. Adrenalin produces an approximate schizophrenia, a drug psychosis. The backbrain is depressed and the frontbrain is almost contentless — there is a complete lack of affect, autism, virtual absence of cerebral events. Adrenalin can look misery in the face and not recognize it. Adrenalin can get knifed in the gut and not notice the hemorrhaging. Adrenalin can beat the shit out of beat-up people without emotional response or interest in the consequences. Adrenalin flattens things out.

He knows how he did what he did. He can describe it flatly as a sequence of events external to himself, sentences in a textbook of self-defence. He pushed himself off the door with his right foot. Hurtling forward, he crashed into two junkies with his parcels. He dropped the bags as he bumped them. He kicked the black guy in the small of the back and locked hands over the head and around the neck of the white guy and squeezed hard and slammed his face into the cindercrete wall. He did everything according to the directions of the guy who'd taught him self-defence after clients started coming into his office with hundreds of thousands in used American bills. Except for *not* doing one thing — doing *nothing* whenever the money doesn't really matter. *A vast still harbour of iridescent water. Deserted gas well flares on the smoky horizon. Stink of oil and sewage. Sick sharks swim through the black water, belch sulphur from rotting livers, ignore a bloody, broken Icarus.* Mugwumpery makes one compulsive. Mugwumpery makes one unstable in relationships, self-destructive, susceptible to suggestion, delusion. *He plummets from the eyeless lighthouse, kissing and jacking off in the face of the black mirror, glides oblique down with cryptic condoms and mosaic of a thousand newspapers through the drowned city of red brick to settle in black mud with tin cans and beer bottles, gangsters in concrete, pistols pounded flat. . . . He waits the slow striptease of erosion with fossil loins.* Mugwumps invent romantic relationships. *The Mugwump slips the noose over the boy's head and tightens the knot caressingly behind the left ear. The boy's penis is retracted, his balls tight. He looks straight ahead breathing deeply. The Mugwump sidles around the boy goosing him . . .* Gabrielle lets herself in with the key he gave her this afternoon. He wishes he understood why she wants him to do the things he does with her.

A LITTLE CONVERSATION, A LITTLE RED WINE

Thierry Montpetit is standing by himself in the Ritz-Carlton Oval Room at his boss's wedding reception when his nobody-knows-what-she-is-going-to-say-next friend from the office Gillian comes over to him breathlessly and says "I want you to meet my mother and say something interesting to her, will you, please?"

She grabs his arm and pulls him through a scrum of guests to her mother on the other side. Her mother is standing alongside Steven who maybe is or maybe isn't Gillian's significant other at the moment but is, Gillian has confided over innumerable cups of coffee at the office, definitely being very supportive while she divorces a husband who is trying very hard to be a sensitive new man without ceasing to be a Westmount old-family egoist, chauvinist and tightwad. And all this would be another story for another time except that Thierry gets the feeling that the absent not-yet-ex-husband is standing between Steven and Gillian's mother and causing difficulties.

"This is my mother and isn't she beautiful and Mom this is my friend from the office, Thierry. He is a simply wonderful storyteller."

"Is that what you do for Robert, Terry, tell stories for him? My brother can't tell a story worth repeating, can he? And then he goes and repeats it endlessly, doesn't he?"

Robert is not only Thierry's boss and the bridegroom but also Gillian's uncle.

"I'm an investigator, a risk investigator," Thierry says as his eyes none-too-privately eye Gillian's mother. She is small, lean, fit, chic, very beautiful in the scrap of expensive black material that serves as her dress. And youthful. The very short skirt goes very well with her long legs. Her legs are sheathed in black stockings and her lips are as red as the string of small rubies at her neck. She is smaller, prettier, more fashion-conscious than her daughter.

"Does that mean you do risky things for him?"

"Good heavens, I hope not!" Has she doubled her meaning deliberately? Is he looking rugged, brave, sexy, fascinating, risqué? "What I try to do is figure out some of the things our customers might do before they do them. For instance, how likely it is that someone who wants to double the insured value of a factory is about to have it burned down."

"Oh, do tell me more! That's so interesting! I always knew that there had to be an adventurous side to insurance. So you're a detective. Do you have to interview these people before they turn criminal or do you have informants among Montreal arsonists? Do you have to keep people from beating up my brother?"

"Nothing so glamorous. I just sift through financial statements. I'm more of an accountant than a detective."

"Oh, please, not another word! I must say I much prefer the idea of you doing dangerous things for my brother. Robert is so stodgy. Look at the pudding he's marrying! Or am I being terribly indiscreet like my daughter? Gillian tells me all the office gossip but very little about her actual work. She does do actual work, doesn't she? Robert doesn't just keep her around for her amusement value, does he?"

"I didn't bring him over to you to talk about our family — or my job!" Gillian says, casting her eyes upwards with a small child's exasperation. Gillian hasn't risen quite as high as quickly in the insurance business as any mother

A Little Conversation, A Little Red Wine

and especially the boss's sister might expect of an intelligent daughter.

Thierry feels pressed to say something diverting but his brain is not responding well. He feels boyishly tongue-tied. Gillian's mother is short-circuiting too many of his synapses. She is much too beautiful to be the mother of a friend who might be more than a friend if she wasn't a co-worker. Thierry is not good at office politics so he has avoided sexual entanglements with the boss's niece. It was difficult until Steven came along. Gillian was very aggressive. It's been impossible not to flirt: she has a great ass, a nice walk, funny remarks.

Steven comes to the rescue. "Mrs. Burton and I were just talking about a ghost that haunts the Ritz — an old rogue who sometimes pats women on the bottom in the ladies cloakroom."

"Are you interested in ghosts, Mrs. Burton?"

"Yes, but not the ass-grabbing sort. Call me Pauline, Terry."

"Actually, it's Thierry. There is an h and an i before the e and a roll on the T," he says softly. He does not like correcting her mispronunciation but he does not like being called something he isn't. Terry. It's only marginally better than being called Theory as Robert is in the habit of doing.

"Tear-ée. Have I got it right now?" Gillian's mother asks very deliberately with a comically French inflection.

He nods uncomfortably. He feels he is being mocked now. Women do not mock rugged, brave, sexy men, do they? Should he have pretended to be a real detective, a private investigator, a Burt Reynolds type? No, he is too short by six inches, too light by forty pounds.

"Gillian's first husband used to wear cowboy boots with his evening suits too. It was the one thing I liked about him," Gillian's mother says looking at his feet. "Are you from out West where the cowboys are cowboys and the Indians are dead?"

The reason Thierry is wearing boots with his charcoal-grey Lanvin suit has nothing to do with his birthplace — which is only as far west as Ville St-Pierre, where the city of Montreal ends and the suburbs of the West Island begin — and everything to do with his back. He'd been bodychecked while playing hockey and suffered lower back troubles throughout the winter, and all the doctors he'd seen were unhelpful. He'd gone to a chiropractor who'd pulled him this way and that in ways that simply hurt an awful lot. After one of those brutal sessions, a taxi driver confided that he should try wearing cowboy boots. Shopping on Greene Avenue on the way home, he'd tried a pair on and walked around the store a bit and the pains went away immediately, and he's been wearing hand-tooled five-hundred-dollar Tony Lamas ever since. His back troubles haven't come back but sometimes his conscience bothers him: Tony Lama uses non-unionized Mexican workers. "I wear them because of my back," he says simply.

"How nice for it and how boring for us," Gillian drawls into his ear. "Say something interesting about cowboys or Indians for godsakes before mother starts asking you about your back problems so she'll have a pretext for telling you about her gynecological problems! Her hot flashes aren't fireworks to anyone but herself. Trust me!"

"My left boot heel has a cross carved in it," Thierry begins.

"And why is that? Does it lessen the risk of being hit by a ledger when you're checking out risky things for Robert?"

Is Gillian's mother being playful now? Or mocking him again?

"To ward off ghosts," he says.

"Let me see."

He raises his boot and steadies himself by placing a hand on Gillian's shoulder. It's a very muscular shoulder, a hard shoulder to snuggle up against, a tough shoulder to cry on. It is the first time he has touched her deliberately. Usually, it's a collision, a bump at the desk, a work-related accident.

"So you really believe in ghosts, do you?"

"Actually, the boot came that way. The salesman thought it was a flaw. I think one of the Mexican bootmakers put it there. Perhaps he had a visit from a ghost while he was making these boots."

"That's really possible, you think?"

"Certainly. Ghosts aren't from another world. Ghosts are very weak dead souls, not at all the diabolical residents of hell they are sometimes made out to be. They're just rather disturbed human spirits, good for a quick fright but not much more, not usually."

"That's quite the theory for an accountant, Tear-ée!" Gillian's mother reaches out and captures a waiter with a bottle of champagne wrapped in a towel and motions him to replenish their drinks. She is elegant and efficient and graceful in her movements. Beautiful.

Thierry sips the thin white fizzy stuff celebrating the married couple and tries not to dribble as he removes his hand from Gillian's shoulder. His fingers tingle from touching her. He looks down the line of her back to the round curve of her buttocks. What would she say if he patted her ass? It is larger, shapelier than her mother's. Steven catches his eye, smirks. Ass. Asshole.

"Has Gillian mentioned to you that my husband is an analyst?"

"Of stocks?"

"No, of bonds! He's a psychoanalyst and that's our little family joke. Of human bondage."

"Is he a Freudian?"

"There's no other analysis, just many ways of wasting time, he says."

"Then you probably know more about troubled spirits than I do?"

"He talks in bed before he goes to sleep so, yes, I do know something of the things that frighten people. My husband doesn't call them ghosts. Or spirits. Nor do I. That's the sort of thing Gillian's father might have said. Has Gillian ever told you about her father? He was a Catholic but not one of the new sort. Vatican II just about unhinged him — he hated losing the Latin Mass. He was very big on possession. Devils. Exorcisms. My husband calls those sorts of conditions 'neurotic displacements.' Gillian's father was forever trying to chase evil spirits from the world with Latin prayers. Gillian gets her mouthiness from him."

Sensing a swing in the conversation that might round completely on her, Gillian nudges Steven and they begin to move away. Gillian's mother says nothing to draw them back. Instead, she touches Thierry's wrist lightly and says, "Do tell me a good ghost story if you know any. I'm less sceptical than my husband."

Thierry knows that Gillian's mother is going to get inside his dreams. Her hair is streaked with silver. Her skin is clear and very pale and subtly scented. He knows he will remember her after the party is over. He doubts if she will remember what he looks like tomorrow morning except for his boots. What can he tell her that will make him memorable?

"My roommate tried to strangle me. At college. My second year. As you can see, he didn't succeed."

"Was it stress-related, a breakdown?"

"When I packed up his stuff after he went into hospital, I discovered pills hidden everywhere — behind books, inside his socks, in his hockey skates. Uppers. Downers. I was shocked: I never saw him take drugs."

Her hip bumps his. "Do tell me the story!"

"It was a very stormy night and the wind was howling, rattling the windows. I was deep asleep despite the racket. I could sleep through anything in those days. Almost anything but not my own death. I dreamed I was drowning. I was going under for the third time. I fought against it. I kicked my legs furiously. I opened my eyes and saw a halo of blue lights and my roomie's eyes a few inches from my face and realized instantly that his hands were gripping my neck and his thumbs were squeezing the life juice out of my Adam's apple. I couldn't roll away so I flung out my right arm. I could barely reach beyond my bed but I got a

A Little Conversation, A Little Red Wine

grip on a corner of my desk and pulled hard enough to wrench it from the wall and dislodge the bookshelf. Books went crashing to the floor. I caught one. I slammed it against the side of his head and he loosened his grip on my throat long enough for me to cry out and then the door burst open and the guys from the next room rushed in and dragged him off me and held him. They called an ambulance and the attendants came with a straightjacket and took him away to the hospital. I had to pack up his belongings and send them home in a trunk to his mother. I still see his face on stormy nights. He's the only ghost I know." Thierry blushes. The story has not come out the way he wanted to tell it. He told it all in a rush like a child might tell its mother. She is Gillian's mother, not his. He meant to be slow and dramatic. He'd failed. She is waving across the room and slipping mentally into the heavy social traffic at its centre. He has lost her interest. He has lost her company.

"I see someone I really must say hello to. It really has been nice meeting you. My daughter is lucky to have such interesting friends." She smiles and presses his hand and swivels her hips and moves away.

Left alone, bored by the prospect of other, emptier conversations, Thierry works his way discreetly out of the reception room and into the lobby. He imagines Gillian's mother still beside him and she holds his arm by the elbow to steady herself on her high heels. She lets her fingers play against the inside of his arm and leans into him and he soaks up perfume and feels impossibly rich as he leaves the hotel and steps out on to Sherbrooke Street. It is a fine, clear evening.

Gillian's mother is still so very much on his mind that Thierry lays out two sets of cutlery and dishes and pours two glasses of red wine before he knows where he is or what he is doing. As he had walked westward home from the wedding reception, he'd thought about the parts of his story that he'd told badly. He hadn't even given his assailant a name. Luc. After the strangling, he'd hated being in that room on his own. He'd wake up in the middle of the night in a cold sweat and see Luc's face hovering and feel thumbs pressing down on his throat. Luc's thumbs. Luc's face. He hadn't given Luc a face. He hadn't described Luc's thin face, hawkish nose, high cheekbones, sunken eyes, pockmarked cheeks, bloodless lips, manifestly false teeth, lank hair. He hadn't said that the thumbs had stunk of cigarettes and matches and were bitten to the quick. As he'd told it, the story had been faceless, weak. He hadn't made it any more for Gillian's mother than a minor incident in a stranger's life.

Why not?

Why hadn't he told her that Luc had been in love with him? According to Gillian, her mother was a woman who was passionately interested in other people's loves. Had he wanted her to be certain about his own sexual preference? Had he really wanted her to want him to be in bed with her, letting him fuck her, letting him work out one part of a mother-and-daughter sex fantasy?

Thierry bites down heavily on a piece of baguette as he surveys the table set for two and the two glasses of dark red wine he has poured. He bites through the bread and into his tongue. *Tabernac.* It hurts like hell. *Hostie. Calice.* He sips a little wine. It stings. He curses steadily, a stream of words that inundate his mind with all the parts of the altarpiece. He hadn't told Gillian's mother that the residence in his story was Le Grand Séminaire and that he and Luc had been studying to become diocesan priests. Did he want her image of him to exclude priestly religion, celibacy? Her ex-husband had been a Catholic. She was married to an atheist now, a Freudian. What would Freud make of his desire to be so very pleasing to the mother of his female best friend? He goes to his stereo and fishes out some Clifton Chenier tapes and loads them into the machine. As the coarse strains of zydeco fill the room, Thierry slices tomatoes and onions, unwraps terrine and

A Little Conversation, A Little Red Wine

cheese and sips his glass of the dark red Spanish wine he loves to drink at home in the evenings. He lays out the food on his table and sits down to his meal. He can feel Gillian's mother in the room with him, seated opposite, all ears, a perfect listener.

"Luc attacked me after the Christmas break in our second year in the seminary. That summer, Luc bought a Volkswagen Beetle when he got out of the hospital and he came by my house and apologized for what had happened and said goodbye and went to live in a fishing shack up north. It was bad of me but I refused to forgive him when he apologized. You see, he was quite obsessed with me. He had a sort of crush on me. I told him to stuff himself. That was the last I saw of him. That was the last anyone saw of him.

"When I returned for my third year, I was assigned to one of the single rooms usually reserved for the deacons. The room they gave me was long and narrow and built into a gable on the top floor. It was so narrow that the bed fit under the slope of the roof and I had to duck my head getting in or out. The weather was hot and muggy and the room was an oven. I couldn't sleep. I started hearing things in the night. They all sounded like Luc. My family's doctor gave me a prescription for tranquillizers. I started to sleep again but I also started getting very cold even though the heat wave hadn't broken. I piled blankets on the bed. No matter how many covers I piled on, I still got cold. It was a funny kind of cold too. It was as if ice was being applied to the soles of my feet. I didn't like what was happening. I went back to the doctor. He told me my symptoms were minor and they'd go away. They were side effects from the drug. He didn't know what else they could be. I didn't tell him about Luc. The weather turned colder. I kept waking up within moments of falling asleep, sensing Luc, cold as ice, in the room. I bought a couple of hot water bottles and took them to bed with me and put them on my feet. They helped some but not enough. I still got cold and the cold had started to work its way up my legs. Worse, I began to feel as if Luc was crawling into bed with me, stealing my warmth. I didn't know what to do.

"I tried talking to a priest, my confessor. He hardly listened. He thought I was complaining about the heating system. Somebody was always complaining about the heating system. I mentioned Luc. My confessor said it was an accident that Luc had attacked me, urged special prayers upon me and returned to the subject of the furnace. Then, one night just as my knees were beginning to freeze, I opened my eyes and saw Luc at the end of my bed. He was holding the covers at my feet and trying to pull them free. He was naked and wet and his dentures clattered in his mouth. He looked very pale, very agitated. I turned on the light and he disappeared. After that I started waiting for him to return every night. A few days later, a letter arrived at the seminary from his parish priest. Luc had drowned. He had been swimming alone in a disused quarry. It had taken nearly a month for his body to come to the surface."

"Are you saying Mass?"

Thierry looks up from the bread he has crumbled between his fingers, startled, confused.

Gillian is standing unsteadily in the open doorway of his apartment. "You were mumbling over the bread and wine. Are you pretending to be a priest? I just found out that you spent three years studying to be a priest! I'm really surprised that you never told me that about yourself! I was hurt until I realized of course it's probably something you don't like talking about very much around work, to women especially, but it's on your university transcripts and one of your personal references. You could have told me, though, because I was raised a Catholic and understand these things."

"How did you get in?"

"You left your door open. I guess you're expecting someone so you can just tell me to leave when they arrive unless you'd rather not have me here cluttering up the

A Little Conversation, A Little Red Wine

place when your company comes. I bet I know who it is, it's the new girl in the office, Tina, isn't it?"

"Nobody's coming."

"No? Do you always set the table for two? I thought I was the only one who ever did that! I do it, of course, so that I'll take more time over my dinner and make it a real meal because otherwise I just gobble and you've seen what gobbling does to me especially when I'm unhappy. Hips like battleships. This is really a nice place you have here and your doorman is kind of sweet. He thought I was drunk but, even so, he let me come up without ringing you first. I told him it was a surprise."

"It is. I didn't know you knew where I live. Where's Steven?"

"There are advantages to working in Personnel. I think Steven's still at the reception. That's where I left him. Can I come in? Can I drink some of that wine? Can I tell you what happened after you left?" Gillian says as she takes the chair opposite him and upends the wineglass. "How can you drink this rough stuff?" she chokes. "Give me a refill!"

"It's smoother if you have something to eat with it. Help yourself to the bread. The terrine is very good."

"So what did you think of my mother? Are you going to tell me that you liked her? I hope you'll tell me that you liked her."

"In that black dress and those rubies, I thought she looked pretty as a prayer book."

"What a great line, Thierry! So Catholic! I'm going to have to remember to tell her. If I knew where to phone her right now I'd phone her and tell her what you said right this instant. She'd like to hear it and know that you said it. She told me she thinks you're very attractive. But that line, it's perfect, it's poetry, it's wonderful."

"It's appropriated. It's not mine. It's something I pinched from *Graceland*. Did she really like me or is that just something you're saying to be polite?"

"You've been to Memphis! You've never said! I've always

wanted to see Elvis's house and his Bibles and his purple velvet drapes and bedspreads. Is it as awful as I think it must be? I'd love to hear everything about it but you should be eating too. This food is wonderful and the wine doesn't taste so rough after the first glass. Like you said, it's smoother with food. And yes, Mom said you are dishy. I think so too."

"Not the place, Graceland. *Graceland,* the album. The Paul Simon album. He sings about the kind of woman I'd want to go to Midnight Mass and spend Christmas Day with. That's your mother."

"You wouldn't have ever wanted to be anywhere near my mother on Christmas Day but that's not what I came here to tell you. Her and her hot flashes! She dropped the turkey carrying it to the table. Who's that singing in French? It isn't Paul Simon, is it? I haven't listened to him in a long time because I like rock and roll and soul and he doesn't do either, does he? Where did he get that accent? What is he saying?"

"No, it's Clifton Chenier from Louisiana. He's singing 'M'appel fou.' Your mother made me feel a little foolish. She's almost too beautiful. What happened after I left?"

"Do you know that whenever it's time to get a man out of my life, there's no place quite like the Ritz? I don't know what that place does to me but it always does something. It just never quits. Maybe it is haunted, like Steven says, by the ass-grabber of all ass-grabbers, the patron saint of chauvinist pigs. Anyway, it always brings out the kind of things in the guy I'm seeing that I don't want to ever see in a guy, so what I came here to tell you is that things got ghastly as soon as you left. My mother took me off to one side for a little heart-to-heart about Steven. She thinks it's too soon for me to get serious with anyone. She thinks Steven is getting much too serious about me. What do you think? Actually, it doesn't matter much what you think or she thinks or even what I think, because by the time I got through talking to my mother, Steven was talking with one of the bridesmaids, who wanted him to come to a party

A Little Conversation, A Little Red Wine

and drag me along only if it was absolutely necessary, so naturally I didn't want to go to it. Then we quarrelled and I could feel from the way he was talking to me that what Mother had said was quite right — about him being too seriously demanding and over-protective and paternalistic — so I told him to go without me and have a good time. I think he stayed on at the reception just to spite me, and now I'm here and yours for the rest of the evening. What are you going to do to keep me from thinking of him? That is, if you're serious that you aren't expecting that new little boy toy from the office to drop in on you! Actually this yummy food is making me forget him already. I think you were the best looking man at the wedding."

Thierry wishes Gillian had a half-sister — somebody as beautiful as her mother, somebody who liked his stories as much as Gillian, somebody who wasn't related to Robert. He likes his job even if the actual work isn't very demanding. It pays very well. Nowadays, he can afford to drink at the Ritz whenever he wants. He remembers the longing with which he used to look at its doors when he passed by on his way back to the seminary after visiting the sick in downtown hospitals. He can afford to buy Lanvin suits at Brisson & Brisson. He looks at his feet. He can afford to have his cowboy boots custom-made by unionized workers in a Québec shop. He doesn't have to wear Tony Lamas. He can afford to put his social conscience at rest. His personal conscience is another matter. He remembers Luc's hand on his knee. It is cold and yellow and damp. He remembers leaving the seminary the day of Luc's funeral and never returning. He looks at the doorway. Gillian didn't pull the door shut behind her. Gillian is chewing slowly and swaying boozily with the music; Clifton Chenier is singing "Quelque chose sur mon idée." Gillian's mother is walking away from the space she has occupied in his thoughts. He gets up slowly from the table, sipping wine as he rises. As he passes her chair, Gillian reaches out, touches his hand, asks, "You don't ever wish you'd stayed in the seminary and become a priest, do you?"

"No, I've never had second thoughts about that."

"What do you have second thoughts about?"

"The way I act in public."

"You have really nice manners. As my mother says, it's easy to tell that you were well brought up."

"Did she really say that?"

"Yes, when she was talking to me about Steven. She was comparing him to you."

"And I came off well?"

"Very well. Please, don't pull away! I like holding your hand."

"All I'm going to do is close the door. It's better not to disturb people."

"Do I disturb you?"

"You're Robert's niece."

"What does that mean?"

"Let me close the door. I don't like being watched."

"I know what you mean," Gillian says when he returns to the table, "it's a problem with Steven. He always wants to be on top, looking down. If I close my eyes, he pulls my hair until I look at him. I don't like that. It turns me off. Do you want to know what turns me on? I like making love in highrise apartments. I like being at least a hundred feet in the air. I like getting slightly drunk on red wine. I like taking a bath with my lover. I like lying on the floor next to the livingroom window with all the lights out. I like my lover behind me, holding me, stroking me, breathing into my hair, telling me that I'm prettier than my mother and nice to be with on Christmas Day. What do you like?"

"I'd like you to hear Paul Simon sing that song. Actually, we should listen to the whole album. It's not rock and roll but I think you'll like it."

As Thierry rises from his stereo, which he has loaded with the *Graceland* CD and fine tuned, he turns back to the room. Gillian is opening his drapes with one hand and unzipping her dress with the other. "If I say that Robert won't know anything about this unless you tell him, is this okay with you?" she asks.

A Little Conversation, A Little Red Wine

"Only if we don't have a bath first. I can't perform when my lover is wet. I don't know why."

Lying on the floor, looking over her shoulder, Thierry looks down upon Westmount streets shaded by great rows of trees. From the height of his apartment on the twentieth floor, his gaze roams easily first to the clutter of the Turcot railyards and then to the jumble of roadways twisting upon themselves at the Ville St-Pierre interchange. Breathing into Gillian's hair, listening to her come to climax with short gasps, Thierry cannot see the street where he came from. At this moment, it doesn't really matter. At this moment, what matters is that he knows the tune and hums along effortlessly.

HORSES

Everett Fredericks needed fresh air, fresh sensations. Friday the thirteenth was unsettling. It started at breakfast when the bailiff served him divorce papers. Sarah wanted a divorce. He knew that. He wanted a divorce too. She knew that. So why had she jumped the gun? She didn't just want a divorce, she wanted a divorce on her own terms. It wasn't going to be no-fault marriage breakdown. Nothing simple. It was going to be cruelty — mental and physical. She was going to make him look bad, worse than he was. Shit. Shit on her. Shit.

That plus coffee plus a searing bowel movement was breakfast. Then there was a rush through downtown Montreal to his college and a broken Xerox machine and a final exam paper that almost didn't get printed on time and awkwardness with his students and that was his morning. Lunch was *steamés* at a *frits* joint with colleagues who spoke of nothing but the inevitability of a referendum on Québec sovereignty. The afternoon was more of the morning — awkward students, uncooperative machines, banality. Dinner was a date with someone he hadn't seen in a couple of years and probably shouldn't have seen for a couple more. His life wasn't the life he wanted to be living. He needed fresh sensations. He needed to get out of town. So he packed a small bag and took off. But not before he washed and dried his breakfast dishes, cleaned his refrigerator, changed his bed linens and read the documents from Sarah's lawyer ten times over and caught a couple of hours of restless sleep.

Ottawa had been a small town with big government buildings when he'd lived there. A decade later, both the town and the buildings had gotten larger. Still, it felt as intimate as a home town at the end of the drive from Montreal. He parked outside the Lord Elgin Hotel and went into Murray's and ordered half a pink grapefruit, two eggs over easy, sausages, toast, croissants, strawberry jam, a bottomless cup of coffee. He ate, drank, ate some more, drank more coffee, smoked three extra-length cigarettes, paid his bill, tipped generously.

The air was cool, clean, clear under a vivid blue sky. Crossing the canal at Laurier, he wandered through the grounds of the university. It no longer felt motherly. He'd outgrown it, passed through more famous campuses, earned higher degrees. As he walked up King Edward, he paused outside the house occupied by the therapists who had once taught him to manage stress effectively. He could use a refresher course. It just wasn't true that he was cruel in the ways Sarah said. He was insensitive. Cruelty was deliberate. Insensitivity was accidental. He lit a cigarette. He wrapped himself in the soothing smoke of fine tobacco, smoke Sarah hadn't always hated. Turning left on Rideau, walking back across the canal, up Parliament Hill, along the back pathway behind the Senate Library and the Peace Tower and the Supreme Court and through its grounds to Wellington Street, he used up a couple more cigarettes and tried to escape Sarah.

His date hadn't been a complete disaster. Last night, he'd learned that he'd lost touch with sensitive new songs and sensitive new singers. In the Treble Clef, he found out who Tom Waits was and why he should listen to Jackson Browne. He bought six albums, including a couple by the Eagles, whose *Hotel California* was *massive* according to the kid at the counter. After that, he went into Sharry's Restaurant and ate a slice of their World Famous Banana Cream Pie, drank more coffee, smoked more cigarettes and made a telephone call that put a smile on his face: the people he wanted to see wanted to see him. On his way back to his car, he bought a couple of bottles of good French wine. Then he took the nearest route into the Gatineau Hills.

Fredericks turned off the expressway and stayed on a secondary road until he came to a farm road that dipped sharply into a hollow. A faded wooden shingle was posted on the largest tree near the road: MacDonald St. Croix — No Hunting. The hollow was soft and wet and deeply rutted from tractor tires. His '70 Oldsmobile 88 laboured mightily, scraping its underside against the muddy ruts, spinning its tires furiously without finding solid footing. He worried about his shock absorbers as he kept a sharp eye out for rocks that might puncture the oil pan or gas tank as he forced the car forward and back and forward again until the road began to grow firmer. But as it grew firmer, the road narrowed and branches of maple trees reached out and scraped the top and sides of the car.

He regretted that he'd not driven the long way round to the front of the property. Now he had no choice. The Olds couldn't be backed up or turned around. Suddenly, free of the trees, the road cut through fine rolling pasture. On the plateau where the road turned left to follow the rim of a bluff, a new truck was parked. He stopped to take a look. Black and shining, it had a pristine white vinyl roof and a creamy white interior. There was a bumper sticker on the back: The Last Frontier is Inside Your Head. It was a rather wonderful truck, a sort of recreational Jeep, a Ford-built four-wheel drive called a Bronco. It seemed more like an oversize toy for an overgrown child than a working piece of equipment for a horse farm. The St. Croix were not the sort of people to go in for mixing up ideas of work and play. Fredericks followed the road along the bluff for another half-mile before entering the farmyard.

A chorus of barks heralded his arrival. It was only a pair of mongrel dogs but they behaved like a pack of wolves, chasing round and round the car as he edged it into the yard. When he stopped, both dogs gathered outside the driver's door and pressed their paws against the window and snarled into his face. He did not trust their canine brains to remember how they were supposed to behave towards an old friend whom they hadn't had the opportunity to sniff in a while. He sat still and waited to be rescued.

Rescue, when it came, came in the form of a low, sharp grunt from the general direction of the barn. The dogs backed off. He opened his car door slowly and stepped out to greet his rescuer, MacDonald St. Croix, the patriarch of the St. Croix clan, who was known variously as "Dad" by his wife and children, "Mac" by those of his neighbours who were neighbourly and "Frenchie the Scot" by those neighbours who weren't. Fredericks called him "Papa Mac."

"Hullo, Papa Mac," he shouted across the twenty yards of bare ground separating his parked car from the barn door. "Fine day, isn't it."

MacDonald St. Croix uttered another low sharp grunt. The dogs came wheeling in on Frederick's legs. He quaked but held his ground. The smaller of the dogs worried his pant leg. He tried to shake him off. The dog clung to him. Papa Mac gurgled with delight and disappeared back into the blackness of the barn. He was left feeling foolish in the middle of the farmyard until Madame St. Croix — whom everyone, himself included, called "Maman" — came out of her kitchen and hurled a shoe at the dog.

"My husband, he has a fine sense of humour, heh. Shame on him, leaving you standing there like that. I have a mind to go out to his barn and give him a taste of another shoe," she said unseriously. Maman was of that generation of farm wives who never had nor ever would set foot inside a barn. Barns were a male preserve. Her daughters did not observe this taboo but that was quite another matter. "You will forgive him, heh, he is an old man. Such an old man. I wonder that I ever came to marry such an old man." Maman was sixty-seven. Papa Mac was seventy-six, but the nine years difference in age now looked like twenty or more.

"Maman, how are you? You look as pretty as ever, and as young. You never seem to grow a day older."

"Ah, if it were only so. I am a senior citizen now, would you believe? The government gives me the pension, heh. Only yesterday it seems to me I was a young girl and that old man out there in the barn was coming to visit my father on Sunday afternoons. And that for sure is a sign that I am getting old. I don't remember what I served the old man for his dinner last night but I can remember the dress I wore that first time he came courting. All my children are grown. And their children, they are growing up too. My eldest grandson, Jean Louis, Robert's boy, graduates from the high school next month. But come in, come in the house. I have a cake cooling."

Fredericks followed her into her oversize kitchen. Maman kept to the old ways. She refused to concede to labour-saving gadgetry of any sort except for a tiny television, a Sony with a picture tube the size of a post card. It sat incongruously alongside the pump for pumping rainwater from the cistern. Her only other concession to modernity was a large refrigerator-freezer, but it was wedged into a pantry beside the kitchen. Maman still cooked on a cast iron range, an old wood-burner which filled the room with the delicious smell of charred wood, an odour further perfumed by freshly brewed coffee and the spicier aroma of the cake cooling on the counter top. Maman laid out three green gingham mats on which she placed bone-handled forks and chocolate-brown earthenware plates and mugs. She arranged a fourth plate and mug along with a large spoon and a heavy plastic straw on a small round wooden tray. Then she cut three large pieces and one small one of her warm cake and placed them on the plates. As she did this, heavy footfalls descended the stairs from above and stomped along the corridor to the kitchen. Fredericks looked up in surprise to see Sylvie, Maman's youngest.

"Take this cake out to Dad and then have some with us, Sylvie."

"Maman! I'm trying to lose weight!"

"Look at her! Tell me, is it reasonable? She is like a sparrow and yet she is always wanting to lose more weight. Say hello to Ti-Ev, Sylvie. You remember him. He will tell you not to be such a foolish girl, heh, I bet. *Vite, vite,* Papa is waiting."

"Hello, Sylvie," he said, taking the initiative. Sylvie hung back, a little unsure of what was expected of her in the circumstances. Her mother clapped her hands to send her on her way out to the barn.

"Hello, good-bye," Sylvie said finally, "I'll be back for my coffee. Don't start without me." She added sugar and cream to the coffee, picked up the tray, strode out the kitchen door and across the yard. He followed her feet with his eyes to see what made the racket when she moved. She wore heavy wooden-soled clogs like the ones many of his students were wearing this season. They were noisy enough on the tiled floors of the college but in the confines of this house they sounded hellish. He supposed that at least they had some practicality on a farm. He looked up from her feet. Her bottom was round, taut, enticing. Being aroused by it was a betrayal of sorts. In the days when he'd been a seminarian in Ottawa, Sylvie had been the darling kid sister of his closest friend, Guy St. Croix, and something of an adopted sister to him.

"Dad, his shakiness — it embarrasses him. Even with his own sons it embarrasses him. Always he eats out there with his precious horses," Maman said apologetically.

"His palsy is worse?" he asked with genuine concern. He liked the old man despite his odd sense of humour.

"Much, much worse. Except when he has a fork — a farm fork — or a pail of horsefeed in his hands. Then he is still like one of his sons. So strong. And Sylvie, she gives him strength. When she is around, he seems to shake less. She is his favourite. A good girl. A pretty girl, heh? But she will not eat. So foolish. Always, she diets. Some of her sisters, they could diet. But Sylvie, she is always on the go, always with Dad and the horses."

Sylvie wasn't long returning. They sat down together to the cake and coffee. Fredericks got caught up on family developments since his last visit. There were thirteen St. Croix children, seven sons and six daughters, four sons-in-law, three daughters-in-law, thirty-five grandchildren, a lot of things happening — but not enough births. "My daughters don't go to church except at Christmas and Easter. They don't have babies every year. They argue with their husbands. The priests can say nothing they will take to heart. Would you believe it, they say they learned this from me. You and Sarah, you should have made babies together. Then, you would not have this talk of divorce now, would you?"

"What can I say, Maman? We tried. It didn't work."

"You should try it again. Divorce is not good."

"I think he should come for a ride with me now, Maman," Sylvie said. "We have just the horse for you, Ev!"

"Okay," he said, out of politeness. He did not like horses very much but he didn't like discussing infertility either. The doctors had never found anything wrong with either of them. They just didn't connect as potential parents.

"But we can't let you go out looking like that. Wait, I'll find you boots and gloves. Guy has some stuff upstairs you can wear," Sylvie said.

He followed Sylvie upstairs and down the long corridor to the back bedroom and waited awkwardly while she produced a pair of green work pants and a checked shirt, a pair of well-worn cowboy boots and an equally worn leather jacket from the wardrobe.

"See how these fit," she ordered.

Fredericks removed his tweed jacket and loosened his knit tie. He hesitated.

"Go ahead. I want to see if they're okay."

He removed his shirt, his loafers, his beige corduroy pants and stepped quickly into the things Sylvie had placed on the bed. She kept her eyes on him the whole time like a mother on a child. The boots weren't too much too big and the jacket wasn't too much too small.

"Okay?" he asked.

"You'll do."

Out at the barn, a bunch of horses were being mechanically milked of their urine. Tankloads of horse piss were transported weekly from the farm to a drug factory outside Montreal. Fredericks wasn't altogether certain what it went to make. Cosmetics? He had a feeling that it might actually have something to do with the manufacture of birth control pills but if it did, no one would say so openly for fear of outraging Maman, who still believed such things were the devil's work. Papa Mac watched him watch the horses micturate while Sylvie saddled him a nice gentle old mare from among the dozen bridle horses at the front of the barn.

"Liquid gold," Papa Mac chortled.

"Jo," said Sylvie, handing him the reins.

They rode in single file and in silence. He was too busy concentrating on what he was doing to make conversation. When they left the woods behind the barn for an open field, Sylvie gave her stallion his head and he sped off at a gallop. The mare had almost lulled him to sleep, she'd moved so slowly and rhythmically beneath him. But at the sight of the stallion's taking wing, some private madness overcame her and she sprang to life, chasing Sylvie's mount. He was jolted forward over the pommel of the saddle until he was straddling the mare's neck. His heart seemed to catch between his lungs. Every breath was a knife stab. He hung on. Once he knew he would neither be thrown nor choke to death, he regained most of the saddle and some rein control. By then the gallop was almost over. They had ridden in a sweeping arc ending in the clearing where he'd admired the Ford Bronco. It was still there. Sylvie slowed her horse and dismounted. She helped Fredericks down.

"I suppose you'd prefer one of these to a horse," Sylvie said sceptically.

"Not really. I like to walk. That's why I drive that wreck of mine. Who does this belong to?"

"No. I wouldn't be caught dead in it. It's a toy. It's Bernice's. Who else in the family would own such a thing? Bernice is living down in the old cabin now. Do you want to visit her?"

"Do you think she'll want to see us?"

"I'll just let her know you're here."

Sylvie left him holding the horses while she climbed inside the cab of the black truck and fiddled with the dials on a CB radio and roared some incomprehensible jargon into it. There was a reply and conversation he couldn't hear.

"Bernice is dying to see you. I'll take the horses back. You can find your way to the cabin, can't you?"

"Aren't you coming?"

"The horses need to be moved around. We keep fifty at a time in the barn for the urine and a dozen for riding and we have another hundred out in pasture. I think that must be more than we had last time. My brothers are in town at the market today selling maple syrup so I have to do more than my share. I'll see you later, I promise."

He was slightly crestfallen. He hadn't anticipated dealing with Bernice on his own. He watched Sylvie mount and ride off. He stood and watched for a long time until she disappeared back into the woods.

The path into the ravine was well-worn and wide at its opening. He followed it easily through the trees down its slope until he came to a stone marker where it branched. The narrower right-hand fork led him to the bottom of the ravine. It was cool, wet, less well worn than the upper path. At the bases of trees, there was still late snow melting slowly and feeding run-off into small streams. He stopped and listened to the sound of the running water. With that music in his ears, he moved forward until he spied the log cabin deep within the wood. It was an old cabin of the type favoured by hunters and trappers: compact, no more than a single room with two small windows, a low doorway and a fieldstone chimney. The door was open and Bernice stood facing the path. She was as small, powerful and rugged as the cabin itself. Her face was from another century but her clothes were not. In place of the long gingham dress and apron and homespun shawl her great-grandmother might have worn and which she might herself wear if she was in Montreal cruising St-Denis on a Friday night, Bernice had on a checked woollen shirt, a sheepskin vest, faded jeans, sneakers. Her black hair streaked with steel-grey strands was pulled tightly into a knot at the nape of her neck. Her eyes were shaded with tinted aviator glasses. She raised her hands to her cheeks in an oddly old-fashioned way and then she was striding over to him, meeting him more than halfway across the small clearing, embracing him and hugging him and kissing him on both cheeks and holding his hands in hers and admiring him with a long, lingering look that ended in direct, prolonged eye contact.

He bent down to be hugged and kissed but drew himself up to his full height under her steady gaze. "*Salut*, Bernice."

"My, my, what a handsome man you still are, Ti-Ev."

She spoke English and he coloured. The last time they had seen one another, Bernice had refused to utter a single word of English. He wondered if his greeting had sounded forced. But no, her English was polished and obviously well-practised.

"You're surprised to hear me speaking English again?"

"Yes."

"Since *Quinze Novembre*, I can afford to be gracious. But let's not talk politics just yet. Let's talk about you. You look peaked. You haven't been getting enough exercise."

"I still walk three or four miles a day," he said defensively.

"Not enough. Not enough. I watched you coming down the path. You have to push, push, push, strive for a better speed every day — and keep your mind free of worries while you are doing it. Think only about walking.

Concentrate on it. Meditate on it. Push. That's what I do and just look at me — a real mess!" She waited for him to flatter her. "Well, come inside, come inside. I have a pot of tea. Or are you too full of Maman's coffee? That's another thing I do not do — drink coffee. *Bienvenue chez moi*, what can you tell me about your life?"

He followed her. Inside, the cabin was dim, dark and his eyes took several seconds to pierce the gloom. Once, it had been his own home, his very first home after leaving the seminary and giving up his intention of becoming a priest. It had been his refuge then and later it was the place to which he had brought Sarah after their wedding. Later still they had come out to it on weekends with Jon, Sarah's son from her first marriage.

In those days, the St. Croix rarely used the cabin themselves but kept it habitable as a hunting lodge and a sort of memorial to the grandfather who had first claimed the horse farm from the sugar bush. Papa Mac and his sons never allowed it to fall into disrepair but they'd kept it bare, sparsely furnished, rustic and insulated from the outside world. In past times it had contained nothing more than a pine table and two rush-bottomed chairs, a long bench, a trundle bed, a couple of shelves for plates and cooking utensils, another with a few books and magazines, and there had been a food locker. For ornamentation, there had only ever been a small wooden crucifix over the hearth. Now, the room was crowded with books, books, and more books — a whole wall of books and thick file folders of all sizes and sorts jammed into a set of rough shelves. More books were spread out over the table and in stacks on the floor surrounding it. All these books fought for space at the table with a jumble of others things — typewriter, tape recorder, boxes of cassettes, camera equipment, slide projector and carousels, slides, pencils, pens, pads, reams of blank paper.

"I'm working on my doctoral dissertation," Bernice said. "It's a wonderful place to work — better than my flat in Montreal! There's nothing here to get in my way. I should have done this years ago. Here, I'll make you Chinese tea and you must tell me how it is with you."

"There isn't much to tell. Term ended yesterday. I couldn't bear marking the final tests and essays so I came here for the day." He stood by the fireplace and played with a globule of wax that had overflowed the lip of a pewter candlestick and spread along the mantelpiece.

Bernice lit a propane stove on the hearth and she set a kettle of water on it. As the water heated, Bernice rummaged among the litter that filled the room. She seemed proud of her disorder. A teapot, tea, cups, saucers and a crushed packet of biscuits emerged from unlikely places and got placed on the long low pine bench.

"How is your research going?" he asked as he played with his piece of wax.

"It's good. It's bad. I'm certain my thesis is right. We do become what we wear. We don't own houses, houses own us. We don't say what's in our mind, our minds become what we say. They hate me for saying this is what sociology is really about. They cut my grant. I survived this year by living in an undergraduate residence as a den mother. At my age! Now they want me to take more courses. You don't want to hear all this."

"Do go on," he said.

"You'll be sorry! When I get going, I don't know when to stop. So they say, and yet they want to give me more to say by giving me more courses to do. I don't grasp their logic, do you?"

"Who exactly are 'they'?"

"My thesis committee, who else? I tell them about the ways in which I can predict ideological shifts on the basis of clothing trends. I tell them that the current fashion for anti-fashion is a fusion of politics, ideology, philosophy, literature and clothing and housing into an interlocking pattern. I ask them to look at what I see and they'll see what's really what. And what do they tell me? They tell me to read more of their books. *Quel dommage!*"

Bernice warmed the pot with a little hot water. As she rinsed it out, he said, "Sarah is suing me for divorce."

"Is this a surprise?"

"I thought we'd agreed on an uncontested divorce — no fault, simple marriage breakdown. Instead, she served me with papers yesterday accusing me of cruelty. You see her in Montreal, don't you? Have you heard her side of it?"

"Were you cruel to her?" she asked as she spooned tea leaves into an earthen pot and drenched them with boiling water.

"You tell me. All she wanted was a simple, pleasant life for Jon, herself and me. She had enough insurance money to support us happily ever after. I just didn't let her spend it. I insisted on paying my own way. I showed her that there was more to the world than a split-level in the suburbs and winter getaways to the south! I was cruel." He watched as she filled the cups with pale green liquid and handed him one. "Thanks." He placed the cup on the mantelpiece. "Okay, seriously, I did do her some harm without intending it. I insisted she look at things squarely and try to understand things she didn't want to know about. But you know Sarah! All she wants to do is to fit into a certain pattern of consumption — eat the right foods, drink the correct wines, listen to the right music, hang the correct pictures by the right artists. Dammit, I should have let her money support us in the style to which she was accustomed and gone berserk inside a gin bottle like the men in her family have always done."

"Why don't you sit down, Ti-Ev, and drink your tea. I'll roll us a joint. What did the divorce petition actually say?"

He sipped his tea slowly. "This is good. I don't need grass but you go ahead. Is it all right if I have a cigarette?"

"I thought you quit."

"I'm forever quitting and then things go wrong and I put it off. That's one of the things Sarah says I've done to her. I've blown smoke in her face. Literally. Second-hand smoke causes heart failure. Did you know that?"

"You're not serious? She's actually charging you with that?"

"That. And more. I made hurtful remarks about her clothing. Bernice, you ought to study her. You should see the way she has been dressing herself! Negative clothing — the nothing look — no panties, no bra, no stockings. Bare everything, so everyone can figure out just what kind of nipples she has and how much pubic hair and how curly it is and how the hair grows in her armpits, so we can forget about all these frivolous things and just pay attention to her soul. Of course I said hurtful things. Who wouldn't? But the real cruelty was that I walked out on her — screwed her in the head. She tell you how I came to walk out on her?"

Bernice inspected the joint she'd rolled and twisted at the end and lit with a match struck against the hearth. "It's no secret I see Sarah sometimes in Montreal but we're not on intimate terms, and when we talk it's in a consciousness raising group that agreed not to talk about men at all, so you've not been mentioned. But she came to one meeting with a black eye and a sprained wrist. Is that what this is about?" She inhaled deeply and offered him the joint.

Fredericks did not want to go where grass might lead him. "It's quite funny, really, what happened. I don't mean her eye and wrist injuries. I feel bad about those. I've never deliberately harmed anyone in my adult life. What was funny was the circumstances. The two of us are sitting at home reading. She's working her way open-mouthed through *The Gulag Archipelago* at my insistence. She's sighing, tut-tutting, trying to attract my attention. I ask her what's bothering her. And she looks up at me as smug as she can be and says, 'He's a male chauvinist and an agrarian reactionary.' Not comprehending, I ask, 'Who is?' 'Solzhenitsyn,' she says. I splutter, 'Is that all you can say of him?' 'Isn't that enough?' she asks. I get up from my chair and try to yank the book from her hands. She holds on so I let go, and she slams the book against her own head. It caught the corner of her eye. She was so angry she wanted to phone the police. I ripped the telephone out of the wall jack and she tried to stop me. That's how she hurt her wrist. But that's not the way she's put it in the divorce papers. Seven years down the drain."

"Seven years! Ti-Ev, dear Ti-Ev, it mystifies me too how you lived together as long as you did. You're not the marrying kind and you never should have married Sarah in the first place. But you can't blame yourself — if anyone is to blame, it's Sarah. She'd been married before, she knew pretty well what she needed, and I think she has always known you couldn't be the kind of mate she needs. But she pretended to be ignorant of herself, her real needs. Probably it was too much fun deceiving herself, allowing herself to be charmed by you. Yes, you're charming, the more so because you don't know what makes you charming. But Sarah doesn't need charm. She needs recklessness, but reckless people kill themselves sometimes like her first husband did. But she had no right to take the coward's way out and marry as safe a husband as you."

"Am I really so very safe?"

"Sarah certainly thought so. Didn't she stay in Ottawa and take a low job in the theology library where she could be so very helpful and so very close to all you handsome God-fearing seminarians? Look, Ti-Ev, I'm sorry. I don't mean to hurt you. You have many, many fine qualities but you simply aren't the kind of person a woman like Sarah should ever have thought of marrying. You need a very different kind of woman if you need a woman at all."

Bernice paused, drew breath, began again. "Try to look at it politically," she said. Her voice was calm, practical as she began to preach. "In a sense, your story isn't very different from the story of my country, Québec. Québec married a safe suitor the second time around. She is rather like Sarah, isn't she? Her first lover, France, was very reckless and uncaring but she loved her. And when that connection was severed, America courted her but was too reckless for her, too male, too given to upheavals and restlessness. So Québec married the safe and reliable old neutered Canada. And what a marriage that has turned out to be! Poor old Canada. Poor old you. You both deserved better but you both married the wrong women. Sarah should have walked out on you the way Québec is going to march out of Canada next year or the year after. But Sarah doesn't have the courage: she refused to take the first move, she forced you to make the break. You can rid yourself of her, you know, you can stop carrying the burden of her weight, her guilt."

"How?"

"I think you first must learn to love the best in yourself, Ti-Ev. Try giving up your job for a year! Put a knapsack on your back. Hike around Europe. Or Asia. You must take a break, make a break with your past. Perhaps we can talk more about all this after dinner. Maman wants us up at the house *tout de suite.* See, Sylvie is signalling." A small light was flashing on the CB receiver. "There's cold water and a towel outside the door if you want to freshen up while I change. Maman likes to see me wearing a skirt whenever a handsome man comes to call," she said with a light laugh. "Go, take the roach with you."

Fredericks stepped outside. The air had suddenly become cold. Bernice had stopped too soon. He had unanswered questions. Grass wouldn't clear his mind. He ground the joint under his heel. Was he getting her clues right? Was she trying to tell him that Sarah was bisexual now, had come out of a closet — at least to women friends? Could he ask her directly? What if she said yes? Could he accept it as nonchalantly as he accepted Bernice's preference for other women? No. Of course not. There were too many things at stake here. He wished he was elsewhere.

Elsewhere. Where else was there? He watched the forest darken around him. Where else was there? He counted off possibilities on his fingertips: if he wasn't here, he would be home alone. And what would he be doing there? He would probably be sitting at his kitchen table, eating a bowl of Campbell's Chunky soup, drinking a glass of milk, chewing on a cheese sandwich made with Kraft slices. He would be grading exam papers and worrying about students who had failed his courses. Was that all that he could imagine for himself? No. Of course, there was more. He could be doing laundry at the laundromat. He could be home reading a good book. He could be in a piano bar quietly listening to Cole Porter songs. He could be watching a movie. But what he would be really doing, whatever else he was doing, would be worrying about the damn divorce papers. And getting nowhere. Here, with Bernice, he might be getting somewhere, somewhere nearer the truth about himself and his relationship with Sarah. What had Bernice suggested? He had to fight off an inner resistance in order to remember her exact words. She'd said he must learn to love what was best in himself. He could be out doing that! What an idea! Loving himself was more important than worrying about how and to whom Sarah was making love. He ought to be a bit reckless, give up his job for a year, hike across Europe, loosen his grip on everything.

"Sorry, I didn't mean to keep you waiting," Bernice said.

"No problem, I was thinking about what you said."
"And?"
"It was very sisterly. You were very kind, *merci beaucoup*."
"Don't thank me, thank the clothes you're wearing!"
"Pardon?"
"You're wearing my brother's clothes! See, what I'm writing makes sense, doesn't it?"

"And the sense I'm to make of the underclothes that Sarah isn't wearing any longer is that she's sort of not interested in men any more. Is that right?" He was surprised by his own bluntness.

"What you must start thinking, Ti-Ev, is that she was never interested in men. Not deep down. If you can see that, she will lose her power to hurt you in your deepest self."

"And how am I supposed to see that? How can I look back on all our years together and see her faking it with me?"

"You can't. Sex wasn't all there was between the two of you, was it?"

"It coloured everything!"

"If that's so, maybe it was the fakery spreading its poison. Maybe you cannot stand alone just yet, maybe you need a woman beside you for a while, a woman who really likes men as men. But right now, you must follow me up this path. *Vite, vite,* expand your lungs, do yourself some good."

She went up the trail twice as fast as he had descended it, a floral skirt swirling around the Russian red leather boots sheathing her calves. He followed as best he could.

Fredericks reached the place where the Ford Bronco was parked and collapsed against it, out of breath. Bernice honked the horn from the driver's seat. "Get in. We'll drive back to the house."

Sliding in beside her, his eyes took in for the first time the changes make-up, a silk shirt, a touch of lingerie, a quilted Chinese jacket and a long skirt made. She looked lovely.

"You like the way I look?"

"I do."

"Is that all you can say?" She slipped the truck into gear.

"I could say you look a little incongruous behind the wheel of this thing."

"You won't say that if you see me out on the logging roads tomorrow four-by-fouring with my buddies. I'm One Hot Mama. That's what they call me on the CB. One Hot Mama." To prove the point, she accelerated as she headed into a sharp curve. "Down here, away from Montreal, alone with my books, I needed an outlet. I bought this. Sunday afternoons I get together with a gang of truckers and we race around the back country. Like you, I need to be more reckless than I've been."

"Really?" Fredericks clutched a handgrip as the nose of the truck dipped suddenly and then rose again sharply.

"I'm serious. I've never been as turned off by men as you seem to think. It's just marriage, courtship, the dating game, proprietorial maleness that leaves me unmoved. I've always wanted to have a baby and I don't want it conceived in a doctor's office with a big syringe. I want to make my baby the way women have always made babies. Sarah and I have come to truths about our bisexuality from different directions — that's why she has my understanding and you have my sympathy. Okay? Did you listen to the baseball last night?"

"I meant to tell you, I had a date. My first date."

"Lucky you!"

"Oh sure, between it and the divorce papers, I almost did myself in. Friday the thirteenth, you can keep it."

"I think the Expos would agree. Chicago beat them 5-3 on thirteen hits with the Expos leaving thirteen runners stranded. It was their thirteenth game at the Olympic Stadium and it evened their record at 13-13."

"I didn't know you took an interest."

"I don't, but you know this family, sports are like religion. Tonight is hockey night but maybe we'll play a little hookey and you'll tell me about your date." She braked and brought the dogs running from the barn. "You can relax now, Ti-Ev, I've stopped."

With a totally unexpected pat on the behind, Bernice nudged him forward into Maman's kitchen and the midst of Saturday night *chez* St. Croix. There was a crush of bodies and a series of hearty handshakes and all the usual wisecracks among siblings and then Maman graciously accepted the wine he had brought before she began shooing him and her sons out of her kitchen and setting her daughters to work preparing food. The men settled into a large pine-panelled room that had been added onto the original farmhouse dining room. It was called the TV room but there was more to it than a large television. It had sofas and recliners and a jumble of footstools and shelves full of board games and a fully stocked bar. Paul, one of the younger brothers, offered him a Campari and soda that he had no trouble accepting. Fredericks stepped aside from the bar and into the outstretched arm of the eldest of Bernice's brothers. They shook hands vigorously.

"So, my friend, has Bernice scared the hell out of you?"

"*Salut*, Robert. Does it show?"

"Bernice scares the hell out of everyone around here, even me! Drink will bring back your colour. My little sister is always the troublemaker, isn't she? I can tell you we haven't had much peace since she moved down to the old cabin. For sure."

"She told me about her Sunday drives."

"Her driving? It's her politics. She won't be happy until she has ruined business for everybody in Québec. Not that you'll be here to see this. You'll be long gone along with everyone else who can afford to get out — all the anglophones, all the allophones. It's only her own people who will drown in red ink once the PQ open the floodgates with their referendum. I'm right, eh?"

"I don't know enough about business to guess what's going to happen to the economy but I don't think there's going to be any great deluge, one way or the other. This referendum isn't going to settle anything except the need for another referendum in ten years." He sipped his drink and eased himself down on to the arm of a sofa.

"So, why is that? Go on," Robert urged.

He didn't want to say more. They'd drawn a circle of listeners. Brothers and brothers-in-law lounged quietly around them. "Don't you think so?" he asked, pushing the centre of the conversation away from himself.

"We want to hear what you think. We're tired of listening to Bernice. Why won't her *indépendantistes* win?" Paul demanded.

"They won't win because they're led by René Lévesque and the federalists are led by Trudeau. It's too uneven a match. Most will side with Trudeau, the man of the world, the man of rationality. Lévesque tries to fudge the issue by arguing for some sort of sovereignty-association with the rest of Canada but Trudeau says that an independent Québec will be a banana republic. The only way the *indépendantistes* have any hope of winning is by replacing Lévesque with Jacques Parizeau, and that won't happen, will it?"

"Not this time, no. But why won't this referendum end it?" Paul asked, egging him on.

"The dream won't die. Hard-core nationalists will have no trouble keeping it alive, because Trudeau will never deliver on his promises — a constitution that reflects the separate reality of Québec, free trade with Ontario — don't make me laugh!"

"But next time — 1990, 1995 — what will happen then? If Québec doesn't get what it wants from Trudeau, won't the shit just get deeper?" Robert asked.

"Perhaps. These people are playing a dangerous game and terrible things can always happen." He wished somebody would interrupt him. They were far too attentive, polite. He looked at his hands and saw the sleeves of the jacket he was wearing. Guy's jacket. Their brother Guy was still the priest in the family, the ultimate authority in the house. No wonder Bernice was as she was! She had to shout to be heard at all. And he had to change his clothes, become himself again. He gulped his drink. "Lots of people talk about the relationship between Québec and the rest of Canada as if it was a marriage on the verge of divorce. Bernice was using the same image with me. I don't think it's accurate. Maybe I spend too much time with teenagers, but I think that ever since the War, Québec has been related to the rest of North America like an adolescent to its parents, and that's much more complex. Think of the USA as the strong father and Canada as the weak mother. Husbands and wives bankrupt one another to settle accounts much more often than children ruin their parents. Will you excuse me? I have to get cleaned up for dinner."

As soon as Fredericks returned in his city clothes, the family assembled at the big table in the dining room. Maman positioned herself at the top of the table nearest the kitchen door and made him take the seat second from her right, next to Bernice, opposite Robert. They were fourteen in all — sons, daughters, husbands, wives, children and Papa Mac at the foot of the table with Sylvie beside him — with enough food to serve twice their number. There was a roast leg of pork and assorted cold meats, two kinds of potatoes and three kinds of vegetables, gravy and apple sauce, jellied salad and green salad, home-baked breads and rolls, all the wine he had brought and wine Robert had made.

"Don't be shy!" Maman urged, "Fill yourself up."

"I'm not shy but I must go easy," he told her, "I have a long drive home."

"Don't worry about that! Stay the night," Robert insisted. "The game will go till eleven o'clock. You don't want to be driving back to Montreal then. Enjoy your dinner. We'll go to Guy's Mass and bring him back for lunch. We'll play some cards. I'll take some of your money."

"That's very kind but I have to be in Montreal in the morning. I wasn't planning on staying for the game." Fredericks forked small portions of pork and crackling on to his plate.

"How can you think of not watching the Habs win the Stanley Cup?" Bernice asked.

"But surely they're not going to win tonight, are they?"

"Certainly. Did you see how they played on Thursday?" Paul demanded from lower down the table. "Wensink said he was going to run Lafleur out of the Boston Gardens for firing the puck at Milbury's face on Tuesday. In two shifts against Lafleur in the first two periods he never hits him once and Lafleur gets two of the four goals and assists on Shutt's and Lemaire's. The way everybody is playing in front of Dryden, Boston's lucky to get the one goal they did. Tonight, we'll shut them out for sure. You have to watch with us! It's history in the making. Why won't they win tonight?"

"I just think they'll want to win it at home in front of their own fans."

"Not this team. They have killer instinct. They want to sweep the series. They want to prove they're the best team ever, better even than the '58 team. Stay the night," Robert commanded.

To his right and down the length of the table, others nodded approvingly. And so he forked more meat on to his plate and added mashed potatoes and turnip and green beans and gravy and apple sauce. He ate and listened and drank and listened as Robert and his nearest brothers went over the Thursday game player by player — Lafleur and Lapointe, Larocque and Lemaire, Mahovlich and Mondou, Nyrop and Riseborough, Roberts, Robinson, Savard, Shutt, Tremblay, Wilson, Bouchard, Chartraw, Cournoyer, Dryden, Gainey, Houle, Jarvis and Lambert. And then they considered Scotty Bowman's coaching. Wine was passed and they drank and he drank and the table was cleared and the wine bottles were emptied and dessert was produced and coffee was served and brandy was brought to the table and all the smokers lit up cigarettes as the non-smokers retreated to the kitchen.

As he lit his second cigarette and inhaled the aroma of the fresh pot of coffee Bernice brought to the table, Fredericks realized that he was now completely incapable of driving himself back to Montreal. He relaxed. He sipped his brandy. It was terrible — almost as cloying as the maple sugar pie that Maman served for dessert.

"What do you think of it?" Robert asked eagerly. "I invented it myself. We have so much maple syrup we have to find new things to do with it."

"You've had a good crop?"

"Too good. Every Saturday, we spend the day with a truckload down at the farmer's market in Ottawa. Everybody cuts prices. Nobody makes a dime. Do you think there are buyers in Montreal?"

"For your brandy?"

"This is just an experiment. No, the syrup."

"I really don't know. I don't go into stores very much."

"Well, we put a couple of cases in your car when you were upstairs. On the back seat. You can give it to your friends. Maybe they'll come out here and ride our horses in the summer, make us some money that way. Grab your coffee, the game is going to start."

It was the end of the first period and Boston was leading 1-0 on a goal by Schmautz on a pass from Brad Park. Bernice came over and whispered in his ear, "Come out to the kitchen. I want to hear about your date." He extricated himself from the crowd around the television and followed her down the corridor. He had never really noticed before the way she swung her ass from side to side. It looked nice — tight, not wobbly. He looked down to her red leather boots and remembered a silly old saying he had heard in a pub in England — *red shoes, no knickers*. He felt an erotic surge. The body truly was a dumb animal!

Sylvie was industriously scouring the roasting pan at the sink.

Bernice said, "I'll finish that off."

"No thanks. I've already got my hands in it."

"I'd rather you let me. I want to talk to Ti-Ev."

"Well, you can wait!"

"It's okay," Fredericks said diplomatically. "We're not exchanging secrets. I had a date last night. My first date since I was married. It was a disaster."

"Who was she?" Bernice asked.

"One of my former students. That was my first mistake. I should have known better but there's no fool like an old teacher."

"You're not so very old!" Sylvie objected.

"That's what Marthe said. Her name is Marthe. I ran into her the other day at the supermarket. We got talking about cooking for ourselves. Her boyfriend had just moved out and she was looking miserable and said she wasn't sure what to do with her life and could we talk on the phone some time and I said 'Why not dinner' and she said 'Great' and that's how I got my first date."

"She was leading you on," Bernice said firmly.

"I was glad to be led."

"She's attractive, is she?"

"A *poupone*, an old-fashioned babe, your trucker friends would eat her up. But very smart."

"So?" Sylvie asked from the sink.

"We met at a place called Bal St Louis over on Prince Arthur, a new place. On the way to the restaurant I was walking by that boutique called Texas Medicine when I bumped right into Sarah. Literally. I walked right into her bare breasts. She's a fruitcake these days. She wanted to try on a blouse that was hanging on a rack on the sidewalk and she didn't care that she wasn't wearing a bra and that the street was full of people. It was doubly embarrassing because I almost knocked her over and then I managed to grab her by the breast trying to keep her from falling. And she kicked me in the shins and yelped before she realized who I was. It was a really stupid incident. Marthe saw it all and so the first thing I had to do was explain a whole lot more about my life than I wanted to on a first date. I mean where was I supposed to go from there?"

"And where did you go?" Bernice asked.

"Into the restaurant and wasn't it quiet, and they served our drinks in two minutes and took our orders right after that, and then Sarah walked in with a girlfriend and sat down facing me at a table maybe ten feet away. We should have gotten up and left but the food was ordered and Marthe couldn't see Sarah so I just let things go. Unlike her, I don't make scenes. A big mistake." He paused while Sylvie emptied the sink and rinsed the roasting pan. The sound of the running water made him conscious of his bladder.

"Then what?" Bernice prompted.

"Well, my encounter with Sarah made me more attractive to Marthe because I told her about the divorce papers and she thought I was incredibly mature not to make a scene on the street. It made her sort of mushy and she started playing footsie with me and Sarah noticed and started making silly faces at me. Marthe of course couldn't see what was going on, and when I started gobbling my food she did the same. To make a long story short, she misunderstood my intentions in getting dinner over real fast. I took her somewhere else for coffee and dessert. I guess this offended her. She went on a talking jag. I heard a lot about musicians I'd never heard of before. Tom Waits. Jackson Browne. It ended up being an early evening."

"You don't know Tom Waits?" Sylvie asked incredulously. "He's dissolute. You must listen to him! I can loan you his latest album."

"Can I get you some ice water?" Bernice interjected.

"Actually, I bought one of his records this morning but I haven't heard it yet."

"Which one?"

"I think its called *Closing Time*. Is that right?"

"Water, Ti-Ev?" Bernice asked.

"Actually, Bernice, there's some water I have to get rid of before the second period starts," he said. "Excuse me."

"You really have to hear his new songs. *Small Change*. They're jazzier, *très cool*." Sylvie said.

"Maybe later," he said.

The game went into overtime. Jacques Lemaire tied it in the second minute of the second period and that only seemed to make the Bruins skate harder. In the third period, the Canadiens had good chances but Cheevers stopped them cold. Then in the fifth minute of overtime, Lemaire took a pass from Lafleur in the slot and drilled it under the crossbar. The household erupted. Cheers. Hugs. Kisses. Fredericks was swept up into the celebration and Bernice was in his arms, her legs pressed hard against his knee. He felt light-headed and a little delirious from the excitement, the drinks that had flowed throughout the game, the cigarettes chain-smoked the last half hour, the closeness of her. He knew he needed fresh air but Robert was pouring a sparkling white wine and everyone was singing and Sylvie clasped his waist from one side and Bernice did the same from the other and the whole room swayed in unison as another brother started them all singing "Gens du pays."

Fredericks woke early, not long after seven; but still it was later than he'd intended. He cursed himself for his foolish drinking. He knew better than to drink that much. His tolerance for alcohol had been low since Sarah and he had split up and his hangovers were more ferocious. His body ached all over. Even his scalp ached. His memories of the night were disjointed. He opened his eyes slowly, bit by bit. It came to him that he was sprawled out on the big iron and brass bed of Guy's room — the spare bedroom built over Maman's kitchen, a room in which he had slept on other occasions. But it seemed that his waking was a reawakening, that earlier he had found himself sharing this bed with Bernice. Bernice had been lying across his chest, enfolded by his arms, naked, her legs intertwined with his and glued to him with sticky fluid. It was not dreamlike, not fantastic, and yet he could not quite bring himself to believe that it was literally true. Even in a mindless state of drunkenness, could he have actually seduced Bernice or been seduced by her? He tried to recover a coherent sense of the night's events, but his memory wasn't very cooperative. He'd watched hockey and there had been loud rejoicing. They'd sung and danced and Sylvie had been on one arm and Bernice had been on the other. He'd gone to bed. He'd begun to undress and Bernice had knocked quietly on the door and come in with Sylvie's record and they had listened to Tom Waits on Guy's stereo. A bluesy piano. A jazzy bass, drums and tenor saxophone. A string section. A rasping, expressive Beatnik voice. The words made him laugh and cry. He could cry — now. Tears for fears.

Fredericks struggled out of bed. His clothes lay scattered in the corner of the room — all of them except his undershorts, which had disappeared. He pulled the bedclothes back over the foot of the bed. He found his shorts in the tangle of sheets. But in finding them, he found something he did not want to find. The bottom sheet was stained with a crusted yellowish-white stain. A wave of nausea flooded over him. A dry heave shook his stomach, then another. Collapsing on the edge of the mattress, his body went wet with fear. He lowered his head between his knees and held it there.

When he got up from the bed, he sponged the stain with his face cloth and water from the bedside pitcher. Maybe Maman would think he'd peed the bed. He looked closely but could not find any loose hairs on the sheets that were not his own. No perfume. He examined himself. No teeth marks nor fingernail scratches. The sensation of Bernice in his bed was a wet dream — nothing more. He was turning into a very strange person. Bernice. What did they have in common? Canada. Québec!

Downstairs in an empty kitchen, Fredericks drank a cup of Maman's thick black coffee. His eyes rested on a rifle that had stood in the corner for as long as he had known the St. Croix. Maman hated the intrusion of this weapon into the peace of her kitchen but Papa Mac insisted on its being there fully loaded, ready to ward off any attackers who dared to trespass beyond the broad limits of St. Croix hospitality. As Fredericks stared at the rifle, he remembered how once, long ago, Maman had asked him to rid her kitchen of it, to take it away and destroy it. He'd refused. He had been afraid even to touch it. He had no understanding of guns, had never fired one. He got up from the table, put his dirty cup and plate in the sink, went over to the rifle, touched it. As he placed his hand on it, he felt a powerful urge to pick up the thing, carry it out to the car, rid Maman of it, recklessly use it on Sarah. His hand recoiled from the weapon, the hate.

Loving himself was more important than worrying about how and with whom Sarah was making love. Absolutely. What had happened between them was over and done with, back pages, a closed chapter in their lives. Maybe a mutual friend could get Sarah to drop the divorce petition. Or he'd simply not contest it. That was better. Bernice had said he ought to learn to be reckless. She had said he could give up his job for a year, hike across Europe. What he really had to do was to loosen his grip on male dominant thinking. On his way out, he paused just long enough to scrawl a thank you to Maman on the chalkboard she kept by the door. As he got into his car, he saw the cases of maple syrup in glass jars that Robert had left on his back seat. While wondering if he should put them in the trunk, he spotted the shadow of Papa Mac at the barn door. He didn't need those damn dogs worrying him. It didn't matter about the syrup. He got in his car and headed out the front gate and back home to Montreal.

Or so he thought. When the rising sun broke through the early morning cloud and hit his rear window, he realized that he'd made a wrong turn and was heading west into Gatineau Park. He wasn't lost, just disoriented. And pissed off at the waste of time. He wanted to get back to Montreal as quickly as possible, contact that mutual friend, get Sarah to behave sensibly. He turned on the radio to a station that featured sports talk and all talk was of the Canadiens' victory. This pleased him. It helped him pull last night into sharp focus. They were running interviews with players. The announcer was talking to Lemaire. All year long, Steve Shutt and Guy Lafleur got the publicity and Jacques Lemaire was overlooked but last night had been Lemaire's night — he'd scored the tying goal in the second period and the winner at 4:32 of sudden-death overtime, and so the Canadiens had swept the Bruins in four games and won their second Stanley Cup in a row. And Fredericks could remember seeing it. It was coming into focus. They'd sung and danced and then they'd sat quietly and watched the awards. Lafleur had won the Conn Smythe Trophy as the outstanding player. They had argued about this, he and Robert and Paul. He and Paul thought Ken Dryden deserved the award because his goals-against average had been spectacular — 1.57 in fourteen games. It had been a gentle argument and then he'd gone up to bed even though the others continued to party.

He'd gotten undressed and Bernice had knocked on the door and come in and they'd played the Tom Waits album. Blues piano. Jazz bass, drums and tenor saxophone. Hollywood strings. An expressive beatnik voice rasping wonderful lyrics full of stories. A Jacques Brel-like story about a drunken sailor on shore leave singing "Waltzing Matilda" in a port where nobody speaks English and everything's broken and he's soaking wet. A carnival barker's monologue full of sly jokes. And then he heard the radio announcer talking to a writer from the *Gazette* and the guy was insisting that this team wasn't in the same league as Toe Blake's '58 Canadiens with Maurice Richard and Doug Harvey, and Fredericks wanted to argue otherwise and the bedroom was forgotten.

It was out on the autoroute near the Ontario border during a break for news and weather that Bernice came back into his mind. They were talking now, continuing their earlier conversation.

"You must try not to be so bitter. Sex wasn't all there was between the two of you. I know it wasn't. There was Jon. You were a really good father to him. You are very good with children."

"Sex coloured everything, even that. The more infertile we were, the more serious sex became. Sex couldn't be good-humoured. Sex couldn't be funny — heaven forbid! It became a sort of religious duty and we became unbelievers. So what did we do? We sprouted *beans and alfalfa, learned how to make yogurt, became amateur wine-makers, listened to all the Beatles' albums from* Revolver *onwards and to Dylan, Cat Stevens, as we painted wall after wall just the right shade of white, macraméd plant holders, stripped and refinished furniture, read* The New York Review of Books *and* Rolling Stone *and* The Village Voice *and* Suck *and god knows how many shelves of meaningful books, attended film festivals and seminars and radical theatrical performances, and worried, worried, worried about countries we had never even heard of before, political prisoners whose cases we knew nothing about, free schools whose curricula we couldn't comprehend. And most of all I worried about all that terrific sex that I just couldn't quite ever manage. What are you doing?"*

He really hadn't needed to ask. She had slipped out of her boots and her blouse and skirt and her hand was pulling off his shorts and the record was spinning silently and she was saying, "This is going to be terrific. I promise."

She had played him like a guitar, touched him in all the right places with her toes, fingers, lips, tongue until the ambivalence he sort of felt when she started just disappeared and she sat on top of him and he asked, "What are you doing now?"

"We are making a baby. I told you I want to have a baby. I want to make my baby the way women have always made babies and I want to make him with you. I want your baby. C'est normal."

"But don't you know that I'm no good at making babies?"

"We don't know if that's true. Sarah never really wanted your baby. I do."

And he had come then like he had not come in a long, long time. He had blacked out, and when he'd come back to consciousness Bernice had been smoking one of his cigarettes and the record was playing and Tom Waits was singing about bad livers and broken hearts. He'd run his hand along the small of her back and she'd whispered *"No regrets now"* as if she meant it. He'd nodded, far less sincerely. He was full of regrets. They flooded in on him. He put his foot to the floor and the old engine kicked into new life.

Highway 40 from Ottawa to Montreal intersects with the 401 to Toronto in a partial cloverleaf. Going into it at mid-morning, he had the sun directly in his eyes. Had he not been crying, he was certain he would have seen the pothole before his right wheel hit it. His shock absorber snapped or maybe it was the axle. The steering column shuddered and shook and the old Olds was out of control and plunging into a field. He was blacking out but he knew he was not dying. Death was sharper than breaking glass and did not smell of maple syrup.

MANON, MUSKOX, NARWHAL, OWL, POLAR BEAR & DYLAN

OVIBOS MOSCHATUS, the sheeplike cow with a musky smell, the muskox is badly named. It has no musk glands. A muskox bull secretes a substance in its urine, evident on its breath during its rut, that is pungent and fairly sweetish, very like gorilla odour. The first Europeans to smell it made an association with musk deer. They were misled by their noses because they were too eager to find riches where none existed.

Closing the yellow Hilroy notebook in which he has carefully copied various details about the muskox from his textbook, Dylan Adler rises from his desk and stretches his body in a highly stylized way that owes a lot to the exercise programs he watches on television every morning. Looking, feeling somewhat Oriental and meditative from the yoga and tai chi he has absorbed along with aerobic dancing before Oprah and Geraldo reign over the airwaves, he glides across his bedroom and looks out the window. Self-absorbed, indifferent to the world, he scratches at the crotch of his sweatpants. He sniffs his fingertips. He realizes that he needs to take a shower: hours of study intercut with fantasies about Manon have raised a stink.

The *takin* of northern Tibet is the muskox's single living relative. The thick golden fleece that Jason sought was the fur of the takin. He too was misled. After the takin, the nearest relatives of the muskox are the Japanese serow, the chamois, the Rocky Mountain goat, the Barbary sheep.

From where he stands, Dylan can see a light burning in Manon's bedroom. He thinks of her sitting at her desk running her fingers through her thick blonde tresses. He never thinks of her hair as hair. He always thinks of it as tresses. It is a word he likes to use in the poems he writes about her. He wonders if he will ever have the courage to show her his poems. Manon Lanois is not like any of the other girls he knows. He likes some other girls but he loves her. He wants her to love him but he does not know if that is what she wants. It is always difficult to know what she wants. She never asks for anything outright, not from him, and she gets confused when he gives her stuff — CDs, old shirts, caps. She is simply not greedy, not like other girls he knows who will take prized stuff from boys they hardly know at all even before the boys have absolutely decided to give it to them. In a few hours, he knows she will be wearing one of his lucky Celtics warm-up shirts and he will be sitting beside her in the same college classroom writing the same test for the same teacher. Dylan knows that he knows just enough to get a passing grade. He also knows that he knows less than Manon will know before she goes to bed. This is the way he likes things to be between them. She comes first, he comes later. This is the way he hopes it will be when they have sexual intercourse, if she finally lets him make love to her. She has a problem about letting him make love to her. He does not understand it. They both had sex with the people they dated before they started seeing one another. He used to think it was just because they had always sort of known one another and had only started dating after he had been giving her a ride downtown to classes for weeks and weeks.

Now, he thinks religion may have something to do with it. She is a Catholic. He is a Jew. He thinks this might matter more to her than it should. He can't think what else it can be and she won't say. But lately she keeps asking him if Jewish men ever get really serious with Gentile women, serious enough to accept them as they are.

> *Oomingmaq*, the Eskimo word for muskox, means the animal with skin like a beard. It is an exaggeration to say that you can't tell which end is which on a muskox without close inspection. Its underfur, which it sheds in patches and streamers from May to July, is eight times warmer than sheep's wool by weight and as soft as the pashm of Kashmir goats.

At his window, Dylan has a telescope of unusual design, a gift from Manon's mom, who had bought it for Manon's dad for Father's Day the year they separated. M. Lanois never used it even once the whole time he owned it and left it behind when he abandoned his wife and daughter and their house in Pointe Claire South for a younger woman with three small children and a large house in Westmount. Finding the telescope at the back of a closet during a bout of housecleaning not long ago, Madame Lanois thrust it into Dylan's willing hands the moment he showed interest in it. It is a fine and precious gift: it gives him the stars in the heavens and the birds of the air and a sense of relatedness to Manon. It makes many things clearer than he has ever seen them.

The telescope is German, the size and shape of a large Thermos bottle, a crackle-coated can filled with several hundred dollars worth of lenses and prisms that can be set and shifted into varying arrangements of extraordinary power and clarity. It has a blue leather case lined in chamois and fitted with irregular recesses that hold mounts, eyepieces, a clock drive and a miniature 35mm camera. Another smaller cylindrical case of the same blue leather holds a tripod. Both cases have straps and buckles for portability. Dylan, however, never takes them anywhere. The telescope is too precious. Every night while other people in his suburban neighbourhood watch David Letterman and Arsenio Hall on late night television or make love or sleep, Dylan studies the world that can be seen from his bedroom window. But right now, he really needs to take a shower.

> A muskox seems to have only two speeds, walk and gallop. It sometimes sits on its haunches; this makes it look thoughtful. It is generally stolid although it does seem to delight in splashing in water. Among ruminants, it is unique in the amount of body contact it makes. At the approach of danger, muskoxen press together, rump to rump, in a rosette which is very effective against wolves.

After he has splashed around in the bathroom for fifteen minutes and used up half a bar of soap on his underarms and genitals, Dylan returns to his bedroom, slips into clean well-worn sweats and positions himself at his telescope, his back to his studies. He is fully awake. Unlike most teenage boys, he has problems sleeping. It's in the nature of his metabolism — a thing much investigated by many different physicians at the Montreal Children's Hospital — for him to be at the zenith of his mental and physical powers during the hours from midnight to noon and at the nadir from noon to midnight. It used to profoundly effect his schoolwork and his father's sex life but now that Dylan has graduated from high school and turned eighteen and started college, his father has decided it's okay to leave him at home by himself.

> The behaviour of a rutting bull is charged with energy. Humans find it amusing and exhilarating. A bull lowers its head and rubs its eyes on the

inside of its forelegs very vigorously as its first threat to another. It then proceeds to rake the ground with its horns. Then, tilting its head, it circles sideways around its foe. This is followed by charging and head-butting of varying degrees of intensity. All of this is done in a stylized way on flat terrain. Bulls charge from distances of twenty to thirty feet apart. When they collide, it sounds like sea ice fracturing. Charges are sometimes fatal to one or both bulls.

The telescope holds Dylan in thrall because it seems to him the very image of the kind of person he wants to be. Once he sets the telescope on a particular thing, it remains fixed on it. It does not wander this way and that, eavesdrop on things that are not its immediate concern. In this sense, it is constant. Constancy is one key to living authentically, he thinks. He has thought a lot about living authentically ever since he read about existentialism in his Humanities course. Correctness is another key, and accuracy is the very essence of the telescope. Its optical glasses and quartzes are ground, rubbed, annealed, corrected, accurate to a ten-thousandth millimetre. Its images are sharp and unblinking. Its camera tells no lies. Constancy, correctness, stability, truthfulness are the things he feels most people lack in their lives. They are not easy to find, focus on, capture.

Right now, he is trying to find and photograph an owl whom he thinks is nesting in a tree in the Lanois's backyard. For the past several nights he has heard its hoots and once caught a glimpse of its shadow on the snow. There have been reports recently of snowy owls feeding outside their normal hunting areas. He is certain it must be a snowy owl nesting near Manon's window.

Manon wants the picture. It is not enough for her that he says he has heard the owl and seen its shadow: she wants proof. So he has fitted the camera to the telescope. He has replaced the in-line ocular with a lateral eyepiece that allows him to take sightings. He is waiting to hear the hoots. As he waits, he thinks about the muskoxen he has been studying. The random facts he has memorized, he realizes, are not the primary facts that his teacher wants him to commit to memory for the test. His teacher wants him to know what niche muskoxen occupy in the food chain in the Canadian arctic. His teacher expects him to be able to say how many muskoxen inhabit the arctic and where they range. But Dylan likes the facts he has gathered. He will tell the teacher these things whether or not the teacher wants to read them. Like Manon, Dylan is enrolled in a community college in downtown Montreal. Unlike Manon, who is a very good student and never skips anything, he attends most classes sporadically because he likes to sit and talk in the cafeteria or just think things through for himself and find his own answers to his own questions in the library, unhindered by teachers. He would not be taking this course with the muskoxen in it at all except that Manon wanted him to take it with her. She says it will help them understand his father better. His father has a beard of almost rabbinical majesty and a very hairy ass. As far as he knows, Manon knows nothing about his father's hairy ass except for the bits that peek out when his father's jeans slide too far down on his hips.

> Muskoxen are warmer than human beings: they maintain a constant body temperature of 101 degrees Fahrenheit. Muskoxen are economical: they expend energy very carefully. The muskox mates in a non-violent way. The males are attentive to the females. A male typically sniffs, chins, noses, eyes and massages a female before mounting her.

Dylan presses his eye to the lateral eyepiece: he has heard a hoot through the open window. The owl isn't where he thinks it will be. He loosens the thumbscrew and the barrel drops down and to the left. He checks the view

and there in the telescope sits Manon in her terrycloth
bathrobe. One of her breasts is fully exposed. The telescope is capable of such clarity and power that he sees the
droplets of water on her skin. Dylan tries to cant the barrel upwards and to the right. It refuses to move: it has
stuck, something it has never done before. Dylan can
scarcely believe the evidence of touch. He squints once
more through the eyepiece. Manon still sits by her window
but her bosom is no longer bare. She has pulled the towel-
ling tight against her chest. He breathes easier. Sometimes
when he watches the sky through the telescope, he'll see a
cluster of stars that looks just like the skin around her
nipple feels when he sucks on it.

> *URSUS MARITIMUS*, the bear at the seashore, the
> bear at the edge, the polar bear has fur like that
> of no other mammal: its outer guard hairs are
> widely spaced and hollow, allowing it to shake
> itself free of water easily and enabling it to
> absorb solar energy. The polar bear is a relatively
> recent arrival in the arctic. It is theorized that a
> group of brown bears became isolated in Siberia
> and evolved into polar bears in the middle or
> late Pleistocene. This theory is given credibility
> by the fact that polar bears and brown bears can
> still cross-breed. But the behaviour of polar bears
> differs markedly from that of brown bears. The
> polar bear is carnivorous and non-territorial.

Manon is bent slightly forward over her textbook. Her
form is deeply familiar to him with its blonde tresses, thick
and long, framing her face. Her cheeks are full and dim-
pled. Her skin is flawless and creamy. She is not yet as
beautiful as her mother but she is lovely and he likes nothing better than to just look at her quietly when she is
studying. He wonders what she is studying at this very moment. The polar bear? He knows that he ought to be
studying the habits of the polar bear. He would like to

phone Manon and ask her questions about the polar bear to see what she knows that he doesn't, but Madame Lanois does not like him telephoning late at night. She says it disturbs her even though Manon has her own telephone in her bedroom.

> Polar bears have a tendency to overheat because they are insulated by blubber rather than fur. They jump in the water or eat snow to cool off. The blubber provides not only warmth but also nourishment. Throughout the five-month period during which a female hibernates, gives birth and nurses her young, she lives entirely on her fat reserves, losing up to sixty per cent of her body weight. In cold weather, polar bears hug their back legs to their stomachs and bury their heads in their chests.

Dylan watches Manon breathing heavily on the window, fogging it. He watches as she extends an index finger and makes lines in the frost. He looks at the thing she has drawn — a heart pierced with an arrow. She is thinking of love. She is thinking of him. Does she know that he is watching her right now? Should he phone her and tell her he has seen her message? His crotch throbs, aches with love. He removes his hand from the telescope, places it palm-down against his penis, rubs it, hardens it, whacks it with a furious gesture. Damn. Damn. Damn. Damn. He jerked off in the shower. He does not need to jerk off again. So soon. But he aches for Manon. She knows that she drives him crazy. She says she cannot help herself: there is just something not right about their having sexual intercourse. Sometimes she feels sorry for him and jerks him off while they watch movies on television. This happens especially when Patrick Swayze or some other muscular hunk is in the movie and her mother is over at his place helping his father pack for a business trip to the North. Manon keeps saying she feels sorry for him that his father has to travel so much this winter, but he keeps telling her he doesn't mind because this way her mom lets him stay for dinner more often. Besides, his father can't help it that the computers he designs for the oil exploration companies keep developing glitches and breaking down.

> The female polar bear dens in late October or early November. She is very particular about the type of snow she selects for her maternity den. The den is often located close to the top of the leeward side of a ridge where snowdrifts have developed. Such a location is unlikely to be buried by an avalanche or exposed by a midwinter storm.

The owl hoots and Dylan jams his penis back in his pants and reaches for the lateral eyepiece. He jars the telescope and the barrel frees itself, shifts sideways, locates the owl. Dylan finds the shutter release on his camera in time, he thinks, to capture the owl before it disappears into the dark recesses of the tree. The owl has moved swiftly but he thinks he has captured it on film. He rubs his eyes with disbelief. He hopes he has captured it on film, otherwise Manon will not believe him when he tells her that it wasn't just any old owl in her backyard but something rarer, finer, a snowy owl. He is absolutely certain it is a snowy owl. It was all white and small, just as it is described in the textbook. He must talk to Manon. He must tell her about the owl. An arctic owl in her own backyard!

> A den is usually constructed with an entrance tunnel five to ten feet long and twenty-four to twenty-eight inches wide and high, a small room at the end of the tunnel's upward slope, and a ventilation hole. Dens are very clean. By metabolizing fat rather than protein, a female produces very little body waste and frequently inserts an anal plug of moss before denning.

Dylan crosses the snowy reaches of his back garden and lets himself out the gate and slips past neighbouring houses with all their lights off and crosses over into Manon's yard. Her back door is unlocked as he knows it will be. He has done this before. He lets himself in and as quietly as he can he climbs the stairs to the upper floor. As he creeps down the corridor, he hears Madame Lanois breathing heavily, asthmatically. He sneaks past her bedroom on tiptoes and lightly taps his code on Manon's door. Manon has heard him coming, the door is open before he has finished tapping.

"What are you doing here?"

"I saw the owl."

"You should be studying."

"I know but I can't study."

"Me neither."

Her room is pink, impossibly clean, comforting.

One to three cubs are born sometime in December or early January. They are blind, deaf, poorly insulated, and unable to walk or smell. Polar bear milk has the consistency of cream and tastes like cod liver oil and has a fish smell. The cubs are so small at birth that the mother can hide one in the rolled toes of her front paw.

As he sits on the edge of her bed, Dylan tries to see Manon as she had been in the lens of the telescope — a person who cares about him so much that she writes love notes to him on her window with her own breath. But it is impossible. She is nervous, anxious, all fidgety now and annoyed with him for coming to see her in the night.

"I wish you wouldn't look at me like that!"

"Like what?"

"You know, so concerned, so wanting to know if I still like you."

"You do still like me?"

"You really shouldn't have to ask. Not now."

"Sorry," he says and means it. "I saw the heart you made on the window. Did you know I was watching your window?"

"I don't like you watching our windows so much."

"The telescope got stuck. I was looking for the owl."

"Get a life!"

"It's true! Totally."

"You were spying on your dad, weren't you?"

"No, how could I. He went out without saying anything. Did he come over here tonight? What did he want?"

"He didn't tell you he was coming over here tonight?"

"No. Why? Is there a problem or something I should know?"

"You'd better wait for him to tell you."

"He's still here?"

"He's with my mom."

"You mean my dad is in the bedroom talking with your mom."

"Get real!"

"What?"

"I don't think they're exactly talking right now."

"What?"

"You know!"

"No." But of course he knows what she means. He steels his nerves and tries hard to think his deepest thoughts about living authentically, seeing things clearly. Seeing things clearly demands courage. But what is courage? His father has killed a musk ox. His father has shot at polar bears. His father has had all kinds of women. Dylan knows that he must think his thoughts about courage with a steady mind and a clear eye but he feels light-headed and Manon is blurring at the edges and his cheek is wet.

"She said yes, so they're celebrating."

> Polar Eskimos call polar bears *pisugtooq*, great wanderers. They travel up to one hundred miles a day, sometimes in a relatively straight line, and have been charted on journeys of up to two thousand miles. The polar bear is a great wanderer

not only because it travels far but because it travels with tireless curiosity.

"Here, look at this! Isn't it wonderful."

Dylan looks at the thing Manon wants him to see. It is ivory — round, evenly tapered, smooth, polished, roundly blunt at the end that protrudes several inches from her hand. Further up its shaft, it is striated in a regular pattern that spirals from right to left. This portion is brindled greenish by a crust of algae. Manon holds it like a dagger and he feels the stab of truth enter his flesh. The ivory is the narwhal tusk his father brought home from the arctic after he last went to the North on business. It is a talisman that he has been hoping his father will give him once he passes the course with the muskoxen in it.

"Your dad gave it to me."

"Why?"

"I was crying, I guess. He said he wanted to give me a present to mark the occasion. I didn't need to be cheered up, not really. I'm glad for my mom. I'm glad for them. Your dad says he wants you to move in with us when they get back. They both say you won't have to go live with your mom in California. We'll be like brother and sister."

"What are you talking about?"

"They really and truly are going to get married! Aren't you glad now we didn't ever go all the way? I mean we'd feel so guilty once they're married. It would sort of be like incest, wouldn't it?"

"What are you talking about?"

"You and me being sort of like brother and sister once they're married."

"What are you talking about?"

"I really thought you were mean that you never wanted to talk about it with me."

"What are you talking about?"

"Your father's intentions. Whenever I asked about Jewish men marrying Gentile women, you'd change the subject."

Manon, Muskox, Narwhal, Owl, Polar Bear & Dylan

"I thought you were talking about us. I didn't even know they were dating. I just thought they were good friends. They've known each other ever since I was six and started taking piano lessons with your mom, you know that. I mean if they'd been more than just friends, he wouldn't have dated all those other people after Mom left, would he?"

"The way you kept coming on to me, I thought you thought he wasn't at all serious about her, that my mom was just another of his girlfriends."

"Why didn't you just tell me plainly what was going on with them?"

"I can't always spell things out the way you want them spelled out."

> The female polar bear does not actually hibernate during the winter. She can awaken and become alert in moments to adjust the ventilation if the den gets too warm or too cold. A bear maintains the temperature at the freezing point no matter how cold it gets outside by radiating about as much heat as a 200-watt lightbulb. If the den gets too warm and begins to ice over, she simply scrapes the ice off.

Dylan has his Walkman turned up very loud but hardly hears the Leonard Cohen words Jennifer Warnes sings over top of the band on *Famous Blue Raincoat*. It is a weird tape, as weird as the mood he's in as he develops his film and dries it and prepares his printer in the basement darkroom. He listens to it and works at his photography so he won't have to talk with his father. He works and replays the tape until his father finally comes to the door of the darkroom and says, "Dyl, I've got to fly down to Toronto for a breakfast meeting. I should be back for supper. We'll get in pizza and talk. I guess we both have lots to say. Good luck on your test. I hope you've been studying in there."

"First we take Manhattan, then we take Baie James,"

Dylan says by way of reply. He does not say it very loudly. He is studying a photograph he took while looking for the owl. It shows Madame Lanois's slippered feet standing on top of his father's cowboy boots, toes to heels at her back door. He is truly amazed that he did not see them clinching in his viewfinder.

> Most polar bears are left-pawed. When stalking seals, they sometimes push blocks of ice in front of them as camouflage.

Dylan remembers this and little else about polar bears and all the other animals that live in the North. After fifteen minutes, he hands in his nearly blank test paper and places the photograph on top. "Is this a snowy owl?" he asks his teacher.

His teacher studies the photograph. "I think it's probably a barn owl — a *tyto alba*. That's what it looks like to me. See, it has a sort of monkey face. Snowy owls as you know belong to the other species — the one without the face discs, right? I can see how you might have been confused. It looks a little too small and a little too light for a barn owl but I'm sure that's what it must be. The way the light is falling on its face, I'm not absolutely certain. It's a good photograph. You were lucky."

"I was watching for it. I had a telescope set up. I should have been studying but I just had to develop it and see if I saw what I thought I saw."

"You'd better run along now. I don't think we should disturb the rest of the students. You can see me in my office later. We'll look at it under a magnifying glass. If it is a barn owl we should be able to see darker flecks in its breast feathers. They'd be sort of cinnamon if this was in colour. We'll also figure out what to do about this test."

Dylan sits in the cafeteria and waits for the class to finish writing the test. Manon didn't look up when he left the room. She isn't speaking to him. He isn't speaking to her. He flips back and forth in his textbook while he waits. It is called *Arctic Dreams*. It is written by an environmentalist named Barry Lopez. It has a lot to say about living authentically, seeking truth, seeing things clearly. It asks the kind of questions he thinks are philosophical even though they are not the kind of things discussed in his Philosophy course. It doesn't tell him all the stuff he needs to know about courage because it's not that kind of book, but it says a lot of things that support his own conclusion that there is more courage to be found in the doing of small deeds than in large ones. He will find himself a small apartment in town. He won't need much money. He will get rid of his car. He will cook for himself. He won't date or go to movies. He will drop his old friends. He will tell new people he meets that he is a devotee of Socrates. They will give him strange looks. He won't care. He can stand alone. Most people are boring. Most people don't know anything about the things that really matter — courtesy, truthfulness.

> In the arctic, owls are not thought to be wise. They are perceived as omens of evil events like ravens in the south. They are signs of darkness and disgrace.

ACKNOWLEDGEMENTS

These stories are fictions. Any resemblance to real persons, living or dead, is purely coincidental. That said, if there aren't moments of recognition, I haven't done my job.

The task of writing fiction isn't as solitary as it is sometimes made out to be; I'm grateful to all the people who read these stories in earlier forms and commented on them, but there are two whom I'd like to thank in particular. Geoff Hancock, the editor of *Canadian Fiction Magazine*, got this book started with a challenge laid down in one of his manifestos and kept the cauldron bubbling by publishing three of the stories. Laurel Boone got all the right stories into the book and the book finished. *Per ardua ad astra*, sez she. *Deo gratias*, sez I.

In "A Hole With A Head In It," the extract from "Mauvais sang" from *Une saison en enfer* by Arthur Rimbaud is in my own deliberately bad translation. The quotation from Norman Bethune comes from *Bethune: The Montreal Years*, by Wendell MacLeod, Libbie Park and Stanley Ryerson (James Lorimer, 1978). The verses at the end are my own variations on the anonymous "A Cowboy's Love Song," collected by John A. Lomax and published in *Songs Of The Cattle Trail and Cow Camp* (Duell, Sloan and Pearce, 1950).

I can think of many bad reasons for reading William Burroughs's *Naked Lunch* (Grove Weidenfeld, 1990), but there is one very good one — Burroughs grasped the perverse consequences of post-war monopoly capitalism faster and more fully than anyone else. In addition to the direct quotations at the end of my story "William Burroughs In Westmount," there are about a dozen hidden snippets that can't quite be called direct quotations.

Facts about arctic wildlife in "Manon, Muskox, Narwhal, Owl, Polar Bear & Dylan" are derived from Barry Lopez, *Arctic Dreams* (Charles Scribner's Sons, 1986), which is an even better book than my Dylan says it is.